Andrew is made welcor
to stay. But he doesn't find the quiet
expected. Conflicts within the household soon make
themselves felt as a battle over his uncle's hobby,
badger-baiting, surfaces.

ANTHONY MASTERS

Badger

To Fay

[signature]

METHUEN

To Rachel who helped me so much,
to Tim, who read and encouraged,
to Mark, Vicky and Simon, for whom this book
was written,
and to Ernest Neal – the badger expert.
Also to Miriam Hodgson for her perceptive editing.

First published in Great Britain 1986
by Methuen Children's Books Ltd
This Methuen Teens edition first published 1987
by Methuen Children's Books Ltd
11 New Fetter Lane, London EC4P 4EE
Copyright © 1986 Anthony Masters

Printed in Great Britain by
Richard Clay Ltd, Bungay, Suffolk

ISBN 0 416 06262 8

Contents

Part One **Townie**

1 'It's only for a fortnight, old son.'
'I don't want to go, Dad.'
'I know you don't. But you need a break.'
'But I *will* go – '
'Good boy.'
'I'll hate it.'
'No, you won't. George Lammas is a marvellous character. Real son of the soil. Not a townie like me. Then there's the kids of course – Jenny and Billy. You haven't seen them for years.'
'I can't even remember them.'
'So here's a chance to jog your memory.'
'What's Mrs Lammas like?'
'Prim? She's a wow!'
'What's a wow?'
'Well – she's full of fun is Prim.'
'How's Mum?'
'She's not so well today. But she'll be all right – after a good rest. She's got to have at least a fortnight with her feet up, the doctor said, or she'll be very ill. You know he said you need to get out of the smoke. You're really run down. And after that wretched guinea pig business – '
They were standing in the dark front of Mr Cooper's junk shop, which was on the corner of the Fulham Road.

BERNIE'S JUNK SHOP –
THE BIGGEST AND THE BEST

ran the legend that blazed over the walls and blinds. There were chairs and tables and battered chests of drawers and book cases on the pavement outside the shop and a pile of old baths and cabinets in the yard. Every morning, very early, Andrew helped his Dad pile it all up. It was hard work but good exercise and when he came home from school he would rush to see what had been sold – usually not very much.

Bernie Cooper had been in business since before Andrew was born. It had always been a struggle to make a living and he was still struggling now. He spent half his time in the shop and the other half doing house clearances. Whilst he was out his wife Margaret kept the business going, but the long years of hard work had finally told on her and now she was completely exhausted.

Bernie went out to the yard and Andrew tiptoed up to see his mother in the cosy flat above the shop. It was the only home he'd ever had and he loved it dearly. His mother opened her eyes as he came into the room.

'Andy!'

'I didn't mean to disturb you, Mum.'

'I can always hear you coming a mile off.'

'Sorry.'

'Don't be sorry.' She smiled at him but he could see she was very tired. 'I like you around me.'

'I'm going to the Lammases.'

She sighed. 'Do you really want to?'

'No.'

Margaret Cooper sat up, looking worried. 'It's just that you've been doing so much for me and

Dad that you've got tired yourself. A bit of country air – '

Andrew swallowed, wondering if they were sending him away because they didn't want him. Maybe Mum would get better faster without him around. But she seemed to guess what he was thinking and said quickly: 'You know we'll miss you, but the doctor said you needed some country air. And you'll miss two weeks of school.'

Andrew shrugged. That made it worse. He wanted to be with his mates not out in some strange country place.

'You'll like your cousins,' she continued hopefully.

'You bet.' Andrew did his best to sound convincing.

'I'm sorry I'm such a wreck.' She closed her eyes again and Andrew bent forward, kissing her on the forehead.

'Get well soon, Mum,' he said quietly.

Andrew felt desperately homesick on the train down to Somerset. He thought of his animals and then felt even worse. Andrew kept two guinea-pigs and a rabbit in the yard and he had miserably said good-bye to them this morning. He had imagined that they had looked at him accusingly, as if he was deserting them for ever.

Two weeks ago there'd been a break-in and the guinea-pigs had been let out. He'd found them terrified, crouching under an old bedstead, shivering. Nothing much had been taken and Dad had blamed it on local kids. Andrew knew what he would do if he ever found out who had done it.

He'd beat them to a pulp. Small as he was, he'd half kill them.

Andrew was small for fourteen, with black, curly hair and a rather pale, narrow face that always looked thin. 'They'll fatten you up down there,' Dad had said as he drove the Bedford away from the station. Andrew wished he could have gone back with him – he didn't want to be fattened up. He would have sat next to him in the old bucketing Bedford truck which kept breaking down. Weekends and holidays he would ride out all over London, clearing houses that were sometimes so spooky and old-fashioned that he would be scared. On the way home, he would stop in lorry drivers' cafés for huge cups of sweet tea and massive bacon sandwiches.

Fields had now replaced the houses and Andrew felt uneasy as if all these big, wide-open spaces would gobble him up. He distrusted the bland, grey horizons and the endless fields seemed hostile. The crowded Fulham Road and the busy North End Road were the only places Andrew wanted to be, and he completely forgot how often he had been bored with those familiar surroundings.

After a while Andrew walked down the violently rocking coaches of the Inter-City train to the buffet and bought himself a hamburger and a coke. He just managed to get back to his seat without spilling them and as he munched and drank, Andrew began to cheer up a little. Food always made him feel better. He started to wonder about the Lammases and what they would really be like.

Gradually Andrew became sleepy as the wheels of the train beat a steady, drowsy rhythm on the rails. Then in no time at all, they were pulling into Taunton. Andrew began to lug his suitcase down from the rack. As he looked out of the window, he felt a rising excitement.

2 'You Andy?'
'Yes.'
'I'm Billy – and there's me dad.'

The stocky boy stood in front of him, his hair a bleached thatch and his grin challenging. Ambling along the platform was perhaps the biggest man Andrew had ever seen for he seemed almost as wide as he was tall.

'Hallo.'
'Hallo.'

Both George and Billy Lammas had strong Somerset accents and at first Andrew found this disconcerting.

'Good journey then?'
'Yes, thank you.'

The huge man was completely bald except for two long blond side-whiskers that went right down to his chin. His pate shone in the June sunlight and his face was tanned and leathery. A pipe was clamped between his teeth and he wore a battered sports jacket and old jodhpurs with army boots. George Lammas was a strange sight but because there was so much of him he had a dignity which his peculiarities could not dispel. Andrew could not

help staring at him, however, for one of his eyes
was a mobile slate grey, and the other was quite still
and stared motionlessly straight ahead.

'Looked your fill, lad?' said George, and Andrew
flew into a panic for he had not realised he had been
staring so intently. Billy's grin widened, as if he was
enjoying Andrew's discomfiture.

'I'm – I'm sorry, Mr Lammas. I didn't – '

But George was roaring with laughter and he
threw an arm round Andrew's shoulders.

'Don't you worry, lad. I was having you on.'

'He lost that eye to a badger,' said Billy through
his father's laughter which immediately increased.

'A what?' asked Andrew incredulously, but
George said:

'Don't listen to the boy. We're a great family
for having people on. Go on, Billy boy – take his
suitcase.'

'I can manage,' said Andrew but Billy had already
grabbed it by the handle. As he took it Andrew
suddenly remembered his mother and tears welled
into his eyes. Desperately he blinked them back.

Shipton was a small stone-built village on the edge
of the Brendon Hills. There was a garage with one
pump, a village shop that sold everything, a cluster
of houses and The Packhorse – the Lammas pub.
Andrew got quite a shock when he saw it for he
was expecting a country pub with a thatched roof
and low beams and benches outside. Instead he saw
a three-storey, square-faced building with its name
painted across the stonework in large red lettering.
The window frames and doors were also painted red
and there was an old rusting tractor parked against

the dusty-looking side wall. The Packhorse was not a welcoming sight and Andrew wondered if anyone ever had the courage to step beyond the dull exterior for a drink.

'Home, sweet home,' rumbled George as he drove his old boneshaker of a Ford Cortina up to the front door. Andrew could hear the sound of violent barking from round the back of the pub as George switched off the engine.

George turned to Billy, who was sitting in the back with Andrew: 'Look lively, lad. Get that suitcase out.'

'I'll take it,' said Andrew, managing to scramble out before Billy. He did not want his suitcase touched again.

'You got something special in there?' asked Billy as Andrew grappled with a faulty catch on the boot. It sprang up, almost hitting him, and Billy guffawed. Andrew grabbed his suitcase out of the oily interior and staggered towards the glaring red paint of the pub door.

It was mid-afternoon and the sun had been quite hot outside. By contrast the dim interior of The Packhorse was cold and there was an all-pervading smell of stale beer and cigarettes. Plastic Venetian blinds covered the windows and Andrew could barely make out the murky shapes of the furnishings. Something detached itself from the shadows. It was the dim figure of a woman. This must be his Auntie Prim.

'Get a light on,' yelled George, and Andrew, unable to bear the weight any longer, dumped his suitcase on to the stone floor. A switch was flicked and the bar was flooded with yellow light. Andrew now saw a small, dumpy woman with dyed hair and a round face that was caked with make-up, making her look almost like a doll. Her lips were a bright red Cupid's bow and she had heavily mascaraed eyes and enough powder on her nose and cheeks to resemble a contestant in a flour-throwing fight. Auntie Prim wore a very low-cut blouse and as she came towards him Andrew could see that the rest of her consisted of a floppy, grubby-looking skirt, bare white legs and tartan slippers. Is this what Dad meant when he said she was a 'wow'?

'So this is Maggie's boy.' She stood very close to him and Andrew felt suffocated. The smell of her violet scent was so strong that he felt sick.

'You saw him when he was a baby,' said George.

'He's lovely,' murmured Prim. The scent of violets increased but underneath it Andrew could also detect the smell of gin. Yet he was not frightened of her as he had been of George. He felt something else – a kind of protectiveness towards her.

'Well – he'll be wanting to see his room, girl.'

But she was still standing in front of him, staring down into Andrew's eyes.

'Prim – '

She started and a muscle in her painted cheek began to twitch: 'Come on – I'll show you up.' She stumbled towards the door and like a flash Billy grasped the handle of Andrew's suitcase.

'I'll take yer treasure up.'

He was grinning again.

At last they left him alone and Andrew looked

disconsolately round his room, his homesickness reaching fever-point. The room was high-ceilinged, with off-white walls and brown paintwork. The bed was hard and there was a small wicker table, a wash-basin and a number of religious pictures.

Andrew went automatically to the window and looked out. Below him he could hear the almost continuous barking of the terriers and saw that there were half a dozen of them in a compound. Small, wiry and noisy.

Andrew lay on the bed, without unpacking his suitcase, and thought about nothing until there was a knock on the door.

'Yes?'

'You ready?' It was Billy's voice.

'Ready?'

'Yeah. We'll take a bite and go fishin'. What do you say?'

'I – yes – O.K.'

'Come on down then.' Andrew detected a rough kindness in Billy's voice and his spirits lifted slightly.

Andrew had never been fishing before and Billy was not the most patient of teachers. The river was very narrow and ran through a small valley with steep, thickly wooded sides. It was difficult to stand by the edge of the water without overbalancing and it was just as difficult to cast without snagging the line on the overhanging trees. Billy seemed very adept and adopted a lithe, half-crouching posture that suited his stocky figure. As Andrew snagged his line for what seemed like the thousandth time, Billy gave vent to a howl of rage.

'You're a bloody fool and no mistake!'

But Andrew, hot, tired, humiliated and home-sick, was not feeling humble any longer.

'Shut up!' he yelled.

Billy looked taken aback. Then his eyes narrowed. 'Don't speak that way to me, boy.'

'I'll speak any way I like. And I *don't* like your rotten fishing. I can't do it and you keep shouting. So get off my back!'

'You want to go in that river?'

'Yeah? Try and make me.'

'Righto.' Billy put down his rod and advanced on him. Andrew stood his ground, throwing his own rod to one side. 'And be careful of that rod,' snarled Billy as he continued to advance.

Andrew braced himself to meet Billy and for a moment they grappled on the steep side of the river bank. But soon Andrew felt himself slipping, so he grabbed Billy round the waist.

'Let go, you stupid – ' But before he could say any more Billy also lost his footing. In a slow, graceful arc they toppled into the running water. It was only a few feet deep and they both gasped as they hit the cold clarity of the tumbling brook.

'Blimey,' said Billy as he sat up. 'That's done it – I'm soaked.'

'So am I,' said Andrew. 'What will your mum say?'

'She won't say nothin',' said Billy. 'She never does. It's Dad you have to watch out for.'

Andrew looked at his watch which, thankfully, was waterproof. It was 6 p.m. He got up shivering.

'Come on. We'd best get back.'

Billy got up too. 'You're all right,' he said. His grin didn't seem so bad to Andrew now.

Andrew and Billy ran until they were too puffed to run any longer. Then they slowed down to a walk on the long, winding road that led back to Shipton between the fields.

'I'm going to school tomorrow,' said Billy.

'I'll mooch around the house, I s'pose.'

'Why don't you come with me?'

'To school? No thanks.'

'You're lucky, you are. Missing school.'

'They gave me some work to do.'

'Bet you don't do it.'

'Bet I do. They'll skin me if I don't.'

'You could exercise the dogs.'

'I might at that.'

'They're a handful.'

'Why've you got so many?'

'We breed 'em. They're prize dogs.'

'They go to Crufts?'

'No – not to the nobs. They got no pedigrees.'

'Then how do you judge them?'

'By their spirit. And how they fight.'

'*Fight?* Fight who?'

But all Billy said was: 'Come on – I'll race you back.'

Slowly and stiffly Andrew began to run.

'You're a couple of varmints, you are!' But George seemed quite pleased with their wet clothes and shivering state. 'Got to know each other, did you?'

They both nodded hesitantly and George said:

'Go on – I'll run baths for you. You're downstairs, son – and you're upstairs, Andy.'

Lying in his steaming bath and feeling a good deal better, Andrew thought about the terriers again. What did they fight? Why did they fight at all? Andrew could hear them now, and from their strident barks he assumed that it was feeding time. He did not feel drawn to them as he normally was to most animals. Suddenly he realised why. They were not pets, kept in the house and taken for walks. They were shut up in a yard and always close to the elements. Andrew lay back in the soapy water and shut his eyes. Suddenly he was very tired.

At supper Andrew met Jenny.

The meal was eaten in a small, cramped room just off the kitchen that served as dining-room and sitting-room. Andrew knew that it was only being used now because he was there. The wallpaper was a confused mass of faded roses, a flight of china ducks climbed one wall and on the other were dark Victorian paintings that showed equally dark Scottish landscapes. The windows were very small and overlooked a back garden that only grew wild, ragged grass, thistles and a couple of old prams.

Auntie Prim was not to be seen at supper and the watery steak and kidney pie was presided over by George. He divided his time between the dining-room and the bar, which was now open and seemed to have a small complement of silently drinking men. Occasionally Andrew could hear the sound of a bell and then George would heave his bulk in its direction.

The first thing that Andrew wondered was how

Jenny could possibly be an offspring of the Lammas family. She was tall and slender, with dark curly hair that tumbled down her neck in ringlets. At fifteen Jenny was very striking to look at and Andrew tried hard not to stare at her pale oval face. She had slate grey eyes with long lashes and a kind of withdrawn look that set her even further apart from her rackety family. Andrew felt attracted to her at once for he had never met a girl with such a mysterious beauty. Jenny did not speak much during the meal and in fact no one said very much at all until George and Billy started an argument.

'Me and Andy are going fishin' again after,' he said challengingly.

George Lammas looked up from his plate and scowled.

'Oh no, you're not. Leastways – *you're* not.'

'Who says?' muttered Billy rudely.

'*I* say.'

'Mum lets me.'

'Your mum's not well tonight. She's having a lie-down.'

'*She* lets me. I'll ask her.' He half rose, but George brought his fist down on the table, making them all jump.

'Sit down.'

Billy sat down quickly.

'You let your mum rest.' There was an oddly tender note in George's voice and Andrew looked up at him, surprised at this gentler side of his Uncle's personality. 'You've got your homework to do, boy.'

'I can do it tomorrow morning,' Billy pleaded.

'No you can't – or I'll have that school-man on to me. You'll do it tonight.'

'But Dad – '

'No arguments.'

Billy stared down at the table in sulky silence. Meanwhile, George turned to Jenny, who looked as if she hadn't been listening to a word anyone had said.

'Well, my girl?'

She turned blankly to him.

'Well, Dad?'

'It's your turn to look after our guest.'

'Is it now?' Her Somerset accent was lighter than the rest of her family's – a soft burr.

'You'll look after Andy tonight.'

'But Dad – '

'I don't need looking after, Mr Lammas. Really I don't.'

'Uncle George to you.'

'Uncle George – honestly I don't need looking after. I can go out on my own.'

'Oh no you won't. We're a hospitable lot, us Lammases. Aren't we, girl?'

'Yes, Dad.' Her face was expressionless. Then she turned to Andrew. 'I'm going for a walk,' she said. 'You'd better come too.'

'You're not going to – ' Billy looked across the table, his eyes alive with malice.

'Shut up, you!' Jenny cut him off in mid-sentence.

'*You* shut up!'

But George was not going to allow them to quarrel.

'Be quiet, boy. Jenny knows what she can't do.'

He grinned at her but Andrew could see there was a threat in the grin. 'Don't you, Jenny?'

'Yes, Dad,' she said again.

3 Jenny and Andrew walked silently towards the hills. It was 8 p.m. and the sun was sinking in a blaze of dusky red. The fields around them were in shadow and there was a stillness that was only broken by the sound of their footsteps on the tarmacadam of the road. Occasionally they heard the distant sound of a car but no traffic came down the narrow, high-banked lane along which they were walking. To Andrew it seemed as if they were travelling along a narrow chasm that grew darker and darker with every step.

Eventually Andrew could bear the silence no longer. 'Where are we going?' he asked.

'Just for a walk,' she replied.

'Where to?'

'Oh – anywhere.'

'You didn't have to take me with you.'

'Dad said I had to.'

'Look – you go your way – I'll go mine. We can fix a time to meet at the pub. Your Dad will never know the difference.'

'I can't do that.'

'Why not?'

'You don't know Dad.' She had paused by a tangle of bushes and for the first time she was looking at him. Andrew saw fear in her slate grey eyes and he began to feel uneasy.

'Is your dad fierce?'

'He can be. Besides – '

'Besides what?'

'He finds out what we do. We can never hide anything from him. Except – ' She paused and then began to walk on quickly. Andrew followed her. Suddenly she stopped again and turned abruptly to face him. 'How can I trust you?' she asked.

'You don't know me. You can't.'

'If you tag along – you'll see him.'

'Who?'

'A friend.'

'You've got a boy-friend.' Silence. 'I tell you – I can scarper. Your Dad'll never know.'

'He will. I know he will. He finds out everything. He thinks I don't see him any more.' Her words were blurted out as if she had no control over them.

'Your boy-friend? That's one thing he *doesn't* know then. That you still see him.'

Jenny looked at Andrew helplessly.

'He'll find out – it's only a matter of time.'

'Are you scared of him?'

'Yes.'

'What about your mum?'

'What about her?'

'Doesn't she back you up?'

'She can't.'

'Why not?'

'She drinks.'

'Oh.'

'But you're not to say.'

Andrew nodded his head.

'And he's *not* my – boy-friend.'

'Who is he then?'

'A friend. And I want to go on seeing him. I want to.'

Jenny sounded like a desperate child and Andrew suddenly felt very protective towards her. He had never had a girl-friend although he would have liked one.

'Can't I help?' Andrew asked enthusiastically. Maybe if he chatted up Jenny she would be his girl-friend. But he knew as the thought danced about in his head that it was all a dream. She was far too old and anyway she'd never really notice him; he was too small and not at all fashion-conscious. Besides, she had a friend already even if she said he wasn't a boy-friend.

'How could *you* help? I don't know why I've told you all this. I can't trust you. You said so yourself.' They stared at each other in the darkening lane. Then she said: 'Come on – or it'll be too late.'

'What do you mean?'

'You'll have to come with me. But if you tell – I'll – I don't know what I'll do.'

Andrew could see that there were tears in Jenny's eyes and said, as reassuringly as he could, 'I promise I won't tell. On the Bible.'

'All right,' said Jenny. 'Come on.'

When they came to a gap in the hedge they climbed through it and Andrew discovered they were in a hill pasture that sloped gently up to a distant copse. Rooks were circling the trees in slow, wide arcs and the sun was still steadily sinking into an orange orb. A breeze blew on their faces and underneath their feet the rising grassland was springy and soft. After they had been walking uphill for a few minutes, Jenny paused.

'I haven't even taken Billy up there.' Jenny's voice was both controlled and determined.

'Oh?'

'Or anyone.'

Andrew's sense of uneasiness increased as he looked upwards at the darkening copse. 'I said I wouldn't tell,' he said hesitantly.

'You scared?'

'Where are we going?' Andrew's voice trembled a little.

'We're going to watch badgers,' replied Jenny.

'We can't talk once we get near.'

They had walked on a few yards and through a gate that was swinging off its hinges while Andrew recovered from his surprise. Now, once again, they paused.

'Why can't you tell your dad that?' asked Andrew.

'Because Dad doesn't know about this lot.'

'What's he got against badgers?'

Jenny turned away from him, her finger-nails digging deep into her palms.

'He sets the terriers on them,' she whispered, and at first Andrew did not think he had heard her correctly.

'What?'

'You've got to come quietly,' she said. 'And whatever you do you must stand where I say. You mustn't speak and you mustn't move. Do you understand?'

'Yes.'

'We'll see them tonight,' she said, but it was as if he was not there and she was speaking aloud to herself. Her withdrawn look had disappeared and she now seemed vibrantly alive. Suddenly Andrew had the strange feeling that Jenny belonged here, with the pasture and the setting sun and the copse that was as mysterious and as dark as she was herself.

A few minutes later they were standing behind some barbed wire just outside the copse itself. The wind was blowing even harder into their faces and Jenny had positioned them both so that the badgers could not pick up their scent. She put a finger to her lips as Andrew's sweater rustled against the rough bark of an oak tree and he was still. There was the honking of a pheasant somewhere in the undergrowth.

For a while Andrew longed to sneeze or cough but soon the feeling passed and he came to accept his body as a shell in which his real self had plenty of room to move. All his senses were alert, and he watched the rooks circling, circling above the trees, sombre against the pale evening sky with its scudding clouds.

A rabbit bounded across the clearing and paused for a few seconds in front of him, its ears flattened, waiting. Then it bounded on, up the steeply rising ground into the darkness.

Jenny stood beside him, and Andrew was warmly, companionably conscious of her sentinel, peaceful figure. He now had the feeling that not only was she part of the landscape but he had

27

become part of it too. He felt no need to move and for the first time since leaving home he was utterly at peace with himself and with the memories of his parents and his home.

They waited for an hour in the stillness while the shadowy darkness crept stealthily in, covering the copse with long fingers that blotted out some of the foliage. Then Andrew smelt a strong, musky scent that was not part of the deciduous smell of the trees and the undergrowth. They were looking down at some holes in the bank that seemed much larger than rabbit holes and had piles of fresh earth outside them. From one of the holes a black-and-white snout suddenly emerged, whiffling at the air tentatively. Soon the rest of the bulky form came out of the hole and looked around. Andrew was rigid with delight and anticipation and he could sense Jenny's excitement beside him. Then, to his disappointment, the badger lumbered off into the darkness.

Jenny's fingers were applying gentle pressure to Andrew's arm so he kept looking at the hole. Something else was emerging. At first, because of the rapidly descending darkness, he was unsure about its size and form. Then he saw that it was another badger, this time a rather smaller, sleeker animal. There was movement behind it and the cubs burst free with a sudden rush, almost pushing their mother aside in their delight at being in the open air. For a while they ran about outside their sett in ever decreasing circles, watched by the mother. Then they began to play, rolling over and over in mock combat with the mother occasionally joining in, emitting a kind of whickering sound that Andrew found both haunting and disturbing. But they did not play for long for the rattling wind seemed to upset them, the noise worrying them into a suspicious standstill. Then they began to root at the ground, still looking up every now and then as the wind increased in strength. After a while, the sow began to move out of sight, the cubs following her, although they could still hear them rooting amongst the vegetation in what was now almost total darkness. In a whisper Jenny began to explain about the badgers, her words like a soft fall of leaves in the blackness.

'Where have they gone?' Andrew whispered back.

'Looking for food. Then they'll travel on for a bit, still foraging as they go. Just before dawn they'll return to the sett.'

'I can still hear them.'

They paused to listen to the sound of the badgers further up the copse. Then there was another noise, a kind of scratching, rubbing sound that made Andrew's hair stand on end.

'What's that?'

'They're sharpening up their claws on the bark of a tree.'

Andrew felt her hand in his and jumped. Jenny was giving him something – a clump of coarse hair which she said was part of a badger's coat. 'It gets caught in the barbed wire. Keep it,' she said.

For a few more seconds Andrew strained his eyes into the blackness, but he could no longer see anything, or even hear them now.

'Come on.' He turned to see that Jenny was holding a torch with a red filter on it.

'Where are we going?'

'We'll move up through the copse very quietly. See if we can get near them again.'

'Won't they mind the torch?'

'They're pretty short-sighted and the red light won't worry them at all.'

'O.K.,' said Andrew hesitantly. 'Let's go.' He moved forward and then paused. He had forgotten the strands of barbed wire in front of him. 'Whoops!'

'Crawl through it,' hissed Jenny. 'I'll hold that middle strand up for you.'

Andrew did as he was told, but then got stuck halfway through.

'Go *on*.'

'I can't.'

'What do you mean – you *can't*?'

'What I say. My anorak's snagged.'

'You idiot!'

'It's not my fault.'

Jenny grabbed at the back of Andrew's anorak, desperately tugging at the barbed wire that was firmly hooked into the shoulder.

'Damn!'

'Can't you get it out?'

'I'm trying.'

She continued to tug until there was a rending sound and Andrew abruptly came free. Fingering the rent in his anorak, Andrew tried to choke back an uncontrollable urge to laugh.

'What's the matter?' snapped Jenny.

'I – '

'Are you crying?' she said as Andrew began to sob from the strain of keeping his laughter in.

'No. I'm – I'm – '

'What?'

'Laughing.'

It all came out in a terrible splutter and Jenny hissed angrily: 'You'll startle the badgers.'

Somehow Andrew managed to suppress his laughter and he helped Jenny through the strands of barbed wire. With great caution they then began to traverse the uneven uphill slope of the copse. Jenny went first, much more sure-footed than Andrew as she strode ahead into the darkness. Andrew followed her, tripping over brambles and roots. Then he froze. Outlined against the skyline was a figure.

'What's up?'

'Shh.'

'Why are you standing so still? Come *on*.'

'Shh.'

'What the hell are you on about?' She turned back and stood angrily in front of him, the torch casting a red beam on his face.

'There's someone up there,' he whispered fearfully. 'Someone standing up there.'

'Good,' said Jenny. 'That'll be Brock.'

4 At last they broke free of the undergrowth. 'No more badgers tonight,' said Jenny in a normal voice. 'You've driven them away – laughing like that.'

'I'm sorry,' Andrew was so petrified of the figure that was standing silently on the hillside that he felt he still had to speak in a whisper.

A warmer note crept into Jenny's voice. 'Don't be afraid of Brock,' she said. 'He won't hurt you.'

The figure turned and slowly began to walk down towards them. The pale light of the rising moon gave his bulk more definition as he approached, and Andrew could see that Brock was very tall and thin, with a thatch of wild hair that tumbled down his shoulders. When he came nearer, Andrew could see that he was middle-aged and his long hair was grey and matted. His beard was also grey and his eyes had great pouches underneath them. He said nothing as he came up, but Andrew could sense both suspicion and hostility.

'What have you brought him for?' he said, sounding as if he did not speak often.

'He's staying with us.'

Andrew could feel Brock's eyes resting on him, and he looked into them with a sense of shock. The eyes were extraordinarily tender and they had the liquidity of a helpless animal. There was something special about Brock – as if all his outward sinister strength masked a great yearning inside – a yearning that Andrew wanted to protect as much as he wanted to protect Jenny. Both of them made him feel more confident, stronger than he really was. And yet, at the same time, they frightened him. It was an odd sensation, and he felt an excitement he had never known before.

'He's all right,' said Jenny and Andrew felt a thrill of pleasure.

The man turned away, looking back at the copse.

Andrew saw that he was dressed in an old army great coat, with corduroy trousers tucked into a pair of muddy Wellingtons.

'I saw the boar come out.' His voice had a tender quality to it and Andrew instinctively knew that he loved the badgers rather more than he loved human beings. Although he obviously liked Jenny – perhaps very much.

Jenny said nothing and there was a long silence. But it was a good silence. Brock's eyes rested on the copse and Andrew had never seen anyone before who could keep so completely still.

'We ought to go home soon,' said Jenny eventually. 'Dad will only start creating.'

'No time for tea?'

'Well – yes. If we're quick.'

'It's made.' The man nodded towards Andrew. 'What's his name?'

'Andrew.'

The man suddenly shot out a long muscular arm. 'Pleased to meet you.' The moonlight picked out the frayed jersey sleeve above the bony wrist.

Andrew shook hands, feeling the horny skin and the warmth that perhaps he only imagined existed beneath it. The man abruptly released Andrew's hand. 'Come on,' he said, 'or it'll be stewed.'

The tall scarecrow figure of Brock led Andrew and Jenny up the long hill pasture and into another, much denser clump of trees. In the centre was a very small clearing and they were soon able to make out the light of a hurricane lamp. When they came into the clearing Andrew could see the dim shape of a ridge tent with the lamp hanging from its pole. Brock went inside the tent and returned with three mugs of tea, a bottle of milk and a packet of sugar.

'Sit down,' he said, 'the ground's dry.'

They sat down and Andrew suddenly felt a great wave of comfortable tiredness as he drank Brock's tea, strong and sweet, in the windy night. But the wind wasn't cold – it simply brought the wood alive with its darting, pattering, rattling rustle.

As they had their tea, Brock and Jenny began to speak, quietly yet urgently, as if they were two army generals plotting a campaign. Andrew listened, lulled into torpor by the tea. But soon he took notice as the talk became more and more important.

'You think they'll come again?' Jenny was saying, her voice choked with angry emotion.

'They were here yesterday night. But the digging was down at Priory Wood.' Brock's voice broke slightly and for the first time Andrew sensed that he was desperate.

'Did they get anywhere?'

'No – too much like hard work.'

'I know he's determined.'

'Yeah – I think he is. He'll be back.'

'What are you talking about?' asked Andrew. He felt both pairs of eyes turn on him suspiciously and tried to meet their gaze. Andrew wanted to be included – whatever it was.

Jenny looked at Andrew doubtfully and exchanged a glance with Brock.

'It's up to you, Jenny,' said Brock quietly. He seemed to share a kind of intimacy with Jenny that made Andrew think they knew each other very well.

Suddenly he felt jealous of Brock and the jealousy was like a hard, hot pain.

Jenny turned threateningly to Andrew. 'If you tell,' she said, 'I'll – I'll never speak to you again!'

'I won't tell.'

'You'd better not.'

'What is it?'

'Well – it's – it's Dad!'

Andrew stared at her. She looked so beautiful in the dark wood that he felt a chill running through him.

'Dad – and the terriers.'

'The terriers?'

'He breeds terriers, right?' There was an edge of impatience to her voice and Andrew nodded hurriedly. 'He sends them down after the badgers.'

'What!'

Jenny's voice shook as she repeated the sentence. 'Yes – he sends them down after the badgers.'

Andrew looked across at Brock but his face was deep in shadow and there was no telling what he was thinking.

'But why?'

'Explain it properly, Jenny,' murmured Brock gently.

'O.K. Dad is the same as the other terrier breeders – some other breeders anyway. He's brought in blood from bull-terriers and lakeland terriers to make the breed more ferocious – or, as they say, more courageous.'

'What do you mean – blood?'

'I don't mean he does it by transfusion,' said Jenny sarcastically. Brock leant forward and touched her arm and she went on in a softer tone:

'It's in the breeding, you see. They mix up the strains. Do you understand?'

'Yes. Sorry.' Andrew felt shocked by Uncle George's cruelty and stupid because Jenny was so impatient. If only she could treat him as an equal.

'So they educate – Dad educates the terriers – by first trying them at badgers to test their courage.'

'But is it allowed?'

'Not legally – no. But Dad's never been that respectful of the law whether it's terriers or licensing hours. Or serving people under eighteen. She spoke so bitterly that Andrew said:

'Don't you – have time for your dad?'

'I hate him.'

'But – '

'I hate him for all that and what he's done to Mum besides.'

Andrew was about to speak but she hurried on, her words now tumbling out in an angry torrent.

'They don't exactly show the terriers at Crufts, you know. After all, they're mixed strains. So they have special shows and I've seen some of the schedules.' She paused and looked at Brock, as if meeting his eyes would quell her uncontrollable emotion. 'They say – they specify – that the terriers should be suitable to go to ground to badgers. Do you know what that means?'

'No – no, not really.'

She looked at Andrew almost angrily and he felt the resentment stir inside. How was he supposed to know?

'It means – it means they're sent down the badger setts, they corner the badgers – and then they dig them out.'

36

'But – but it's so cruel.'

'Of course it's cruel. But that's not the end to it.'

'What else?' Andrew's voice was trembling now.

'They take the badgers. One or two of them and leave the cubs. Sport for another year – except they may die.'

The picture of the copse was in Andrew's mind.

'Where do they take them?'

'To back yards – and then they make the badgers fight the terriers. Bets are taken on the results.'

'Who usually wins?'

'Neither. They both end up in a filthy mess. But the badger usually dies.'

'Of his wounds?'

'Not always. I think he dies of a broken heart.'

There was a short silence.

'You mean Uncle George does this?' said Andrew chokingly. He could hardly believe it.

'*And* his friends. They call it a sport.'

'Billy?'

'They take him too. He loves it.'

'It's horrible.'

'And now they've been in Priory Wood digging. Soon they'll be up here.'

'Can't you stop them?'

'I've tried. They just laugh at me. They took me once – it was horrible. That's how I came up here to watch them on my own. And met Brock. Of course he found out.'

'Uncle George?'

'He said if I saw Brock again he'd call the police. So I sneak out now.'

'But why does Uncle George hate you so?' asked Andrew turning to Brock.

'That's a long story,' he replied. 'Not worth going into now.'

'But can't you call the police? If it's illegal surely the police will stop them.'

Brock suddenly spoke. 'That's already been tried.'

'What happened?'

'The police say they haven't got time to put surveillance on badger setts.'

'Brock lives here,' said Jenny, changing the subject.

'I used to be a bit of a hermit,' said Brock, sounding as if he was laughing at her. 'There's no work – leastways not much. The farmer lets me live up here in return for a few odd jobs. No use me talking to the police. I'm not the kind of bloke to impress them, you know. Far from it.'

Suddenly Andrew saw another side of Brock, a warm, intelligent self-mocking side. He was very human then – and he felt drawn to him, almost wanted to protect him. Brock was a loner and maybe he was as in as much danger as the badgers.

'Uncle George and Billy – they couldn't be so cruel,' said Andrew vehemently, feeling thoroughly disillusioned with them.

'They say it's a sport – they're getting rid of a pest.'

'But they're not pests, are they?' Andrew turned to Brock.

'No. But some farmers think they kill lambs and spread T.B. to cattle.'

'And do they?'

'They're all right,' said Brock getting up. There was a hard note to his voice.

38

'Can't *I* speak to them?'

'To the police?' Jenny laughed.

'No – to Uncle George – and Billy.'

Jenny turned on him fiercely. 'If you do,' she said, 'Dad'll know I've been seeing the badgers again, and Brock.'

'What'll happen?'

'He'll beat me. And ban me from going out. He'll keep me in – like a prisoner.'

'So we can't do anything,' said Andrew miserably. 'They'll dig up the copse.'

'No they won't,' said Brock suddenly, with a quietness that Andrew found frightening.

There was a pause.

'You must get back now,' Brock said.

'But we haven't decided anything,' Jenny protested.

Brock raised a hand in protest. 'I've told you, I'll make sure they don't come here. Now, you *must* go.'

'Come on,' said Jenny, 'we'll have to run back.' She stood up, hauled Andrew to his feet and began to drag him through the trees.

'How will he stop Uncle George?' Andrew puffed as they ran down the hillside.

'I don't know. He will. Now come *on*.' They ran past the badger copse and Andrew imagined the boar out there, rooting away, while perhaps his family had resumed their foraging.

'You mustn't tell,' came Jenny's voice, rent on the wind.

'I won't,' said Andrew. 'I promise I won't.' He felt both angry about the badgers and anxious to please Jenny. As she ran in front of him she looked like a will o' the wisp – a sort of half-human, half-fairy figure he had once seen in an old picture book.

They ran on through the night.

5 Uncle George was furious when they got back and Jenny immediately said they had gone to the fair at Shipton. The lie did not quench his anger, or the fury of Billy, who had only just finished his homework.

'I hope you haven't been where I think you've been,' raged Uncle George, standing an inch from Jenny's face.

'I told you – we've been to the fair.'

'Do you *know* what the time is?'

'Don't believe her, Dad. She's been up with that old man.'

'It's past eleven. Past closing time.'

'That dirty old man,' Billy hissed.

'The *bar's* closed.'

'He's not a dirty old man, so shut up, you.'

'Dirty old man! Dirty old man!'

'I'll break your bloody little neck.'

'Shut up, Billy.' Uncle George turned on him.

'Dad, it's not me who comes in late.'

'I said, shut up.'

During the row Andrew stood back in the brightly lit kitchen, realising that the others had forgotten he was there. He felt exhausted and only wanted to go to bed, but Uncle George was still determined to harangue Jenny.

'I want the truth, my girl.'

'The truth is we went to the fair. Didn't we, Andrew?'

Now appealed to, Andrew felt as if he was flushing red in the face. He strove to sound confident.

'Yes, it was great. Sorry we're late.'

Uncle George looked at him as if he could see inside his mind. Then he seemed to make up his own.

'All right. I'll believe you. Thousands wouldn't. But listen to me, Andy, while you're staying with us you've got to obey the house rules. And that means bed before eleven. Yes?'

'Yes, Uncle George.'

He turned back to Jenny. 'And you ought to know better.'

'Yes, Dad.'

'Leading Andrew astray. Still, I'll say no more. But I'll give you a warning, girl. Don't try to play stupid with me, will you? Not ever again.'

'No, Dad.'

Uncle George turned back to the entrance of the empty bar, a drying-up cloth over his arm. 'Your mum hasn't been well tonight, so you can see what I have to put up with,' he muttered.

That night Andrew lay awake, thinking about Jenny and how much he wanted to help her. He wondered about Brock – where he came from and what he was doing living as a hermit in the woods. But his thoughts continuously returned to Jenny and he kept seeing her face in his mind's eye, full of angry passion. He wanted to protect her and the badgers.

The next morning Andrew slept in late. When he got up The Packhorse seemed deserted, with the terriers howling in the yard. It was ten o'clock and Billy and Jenny were obviously at school. But where was Uncle George and Auntie Prim? Wasn't there going to be any breakfast for him? As he walked disconsolately through the empty kitchen, he heard a shuffling on the stairs and for a moment he felt a thrill of fear. Andrew was reminded of a horror film he had recently seen on TV. What was it called? Oh yes, *The Tread on the Stair*.

But it was only his aunt who came into view, her puffy face once again inexpertly caked with make-up. She was wearing an old dressing-gown and her tartan slippers and did not look as if she had break-fast in mind at all.

'Hallo, Auntie Prim.'

She stared at him blankly as if she did not know who he was. Then she remembered and smiled engagingly through her cracked make-up. It was an extraordinary smile and Andrew was reminded of the way a very young child smiles.

'Hallo, darling.' Auntie Prim's voice was expressionless.

'Any breakfast?' he asked, taking the law into his own hands.

'Breakfast?' She repeated the word as if she had not heard it before. Then Auntie Prim blinked and seemed to adjust to the bright morning light. 'I'll get you some breakfast.'

She hard-boiled an egg for him, burnt the toast

and gave him a cup of stewed tea. But Andrew was so hungry that he ate it up, hardly noticing how bad it all was. As he ate, she sat beside him at the table. She looked ill and several times she closed her eyes.

'Are you all right, Auntie?' asked Andrew as he spread marmalade over his second slice of burnt toast.

She stared across at him, suddenly giving him a half-smile. 'Just tired,' she said.

The terriers were still making a good deal of noise and Andrew wondered if they kept barking all day. Who exercised them, he wondered, and when?

'Where's Uncle George?'

'Gone to market. Wanted to get a couple of sides of bacon.'

'Oh.' There seemed nothing else to say. Andrew finished his toast and then saw his torn anorak hanging over the ancient kitchen range. 'I'll go for a walk,' he said, getting up.

'Wait a moment.' Suddenly she seemed much more alert and Andrew stared at her in surprise.

'Sit down a minute, lad. Want some more tea?'

'No thanks.'

'Stewed, was it?'

'No, it was fine.'

'It was stewed.' She stared at him for a moment and then fumbled in her dressing-gown pocket for a cigarette. Having smoked for a few seconds in silence, as if she was making up her mind about something, Auntie Prim said: 'You're a nice lad.'

Andrew felt he should say something in reply but her strange alertness made him wary.

'Jenny and my husband – they don't see eye to eye.'

Again Andrew said nothing and Auntie Prim continued to draw at her cigarette.

'Your mum's my sister,' she said flatly.

'I know,' said Andrew. Was she daft or something?

'She's all right, is Maggie.'

There was a long silence.

'Now me, I'm not so lucky. I've been ill.'

There was another silence then Auntie Prim added: 'There was a time – before I got ill – when George and Jenny were just like that.' She crossed her fingers and suddenly looked at Andrew. 'Know what I mean?'

'They got on all right.'

'They did – then.'

'Why don't they get on now?'

'Oh, she's got her secrets, she has. Growing up, you see. Billy's his boy now. But he and Jenny used to be as thick as thieves – before I got ill. Jenny takes her mum's side now, though I say there's no need. But you be careful if you go gallivanting with her. She got mixed up with a travellin' feller. Nothing – nasty, see. Just got mixed up – and her dad – he was livid.'

If anyone's mixed up, thought Andrew, it's you. There was a strange smile on her face as if she was playing a game with him. Hopefully he stood up again.

'I – I'll go for a walk now.'

'What?' She looked startled, as if she could not cope with sudden movement.

'I'll just go out for a bit.'

44

'No.' Her voice sounded almost pleading, as if she could not bear to be left alone.

'But – '

'Your Uncle George wants you to help with the dogs. He'll be back soon. You sit down and talk to me. How's your mum?'

Very reluctantly Andrew sat down, feeling depressed again. Ever since the badgers and the expedition last night he had felt a sense of elation and excitement which had covered up his homesickness. But now, trapped with his aunt, he felt – well, not homesick exactly but certainly miserable. Then he thought of Jenny and his spirits rose a little.

'She's not well,' he said baldly.

'Tired, is she?'

'That's why I've come down – ' But before Andrew could finish, he could hear the roar of a truck as it stopped outside The Packhorse.

'That'll be him.'

'Uncle George?'

'Now, you be careful. No secrets, eh? My husband doesn't like secrets.' This time there was a hint of a threat in her voice.

Andrew said nothing as he listened to the truck engine being switched off and Uncle George's boots crunching into the yard. The dogs set up an even greater howling as he passed them and threw open the kitchen door.

'Morning, Andy.'

'Morning, Uncle George.'

The big mountain of a man seemed in a good mood as he stumped in, ignoring Auntie Prim and swinging a friendly punch in Andrew's direction. Andrew looked at the enormous ham fist and tried to imagine what the punch would be like if his uncle were not so friendly.

'Had your breakfast, boy?'

'Thanks.'

'Well you want to keep occupied down here. Specially with Billy in school. Want to take the dogs out?'

'On my own?' Andrew looked alarmed. It was the last thing he wanted to do.

Uncle George chuckled. 'They're too much of a handful for a lad. I load 'em in the truck and take 'em up Priory Wood.'

Andrew froze. Priory Wood – that was the place Jenny and Brock had been talking about last night – where Uncle George and his friends had been digging for badgers.

'Well, going to come and give me a hand?' His dead eye seemed fixed on him relentlessly.

'Yes,' said Andrew hastily. ''Course I will.'

'Good lad. Get your anorak and we'll go.'

All this time Uncle George had not given his wife the slightest glance. It was as if he was entirely uninterested in her.

Andrew went to the range, lifted off his anorak and put it on. Uncle George grinned at him.

Andrew put his hand in the pocket to see if his pen-knife was still there. It was, but wrapped round it was a bit of paper.

'You ready?'

'I'll just go to the toilet.'

'Righto, lad.'

Andrew went into the cramped, musty little toilet that led off the kitchen, took out the piece of paper and sat on the seat to read it. It was from Jenny.

Dear Andrew,

Thanks for keeping up the fairy story.
Dad hates Brock and the badgers and if
he had his way, he'd kill them all. But
we're not going to let him. I like you – I
didn't think I was going to.

Yours sincerely,
Jenny

Andrew felt a warm glow of contentment as he
began to read the note for the second time. He also
felt the new excitement beginning to burn inside
him again.

Priory Wood did not seem to be in the same direction as the copse and Andrew felt a sense of relief
as the old Bedford truck thumped along a rutted
lane that climbed the sharply rising ground of the
wood. Alongside the track was a rubbish dump.

'Filthy mess,' said Uncle George as he clutched
the bucketing wheel. 'A real filthy mess that is.'

They eventually reached the lay-by and the truck
came to a juddering standstill. The yelping of the
terriers inside intensified.

'They can smell rats,' said Uncle George, lighting
a pipe.

'Rats – in a wood?'

'They live off the rubbish. Good rat-hunting
country. Come on.'

For such a big man he moved lithely out of the
driver's seat and jumped to the ground. Andrew
joined him as he went to the tailboard and rattled it
down. The small brown-and-white terriers bounded
out, jumping up and down around Uncle George's

ankles. Laughingly he stroked and petted them, and Andrew saw how gentle his great hands were as he played with the terriers.

'What are their names?' asked Andrew.

'Trouncer, Trapper, Tasher, Tackler and Trouble. They're all from the same litter.' Uncle George seemed genuinely delighted that Andrew was interested and the little dogs licked at his calloused palms. 'I love 'em – they're my life, you know.'

'What funny names!'

'They're little show dogs. I show 'em all over the country – and they've won some prizes. I'm real proud of this lot.'

'Does Billy like them?'

'Loves 'em – like me. It's the women who aren't interested. Course, the wife's not herself. And Jenny – well, she's Jenny.' Uncle George sighed and Andrew was shocked to see tears in his uncle's eyes.

'Why's he called Trapper?'

Uncle George cleared his throat loudly and looked away. He answered vaguely: 'Because he's a good little worrier.'

'What does he worry at?'

'They're trained to run badgers to earth,' said Uncle George with sudden enthusiasm. 'That's how we get 'em up to show standards, see. Running old Brock to earth.'

Andrew shivered in the warm confines of the noon-day wood.

'What's up, lad?'

'Nothing.'

'Haven't caught a cold, lad, have you? After your duckin'?'

48

Andrew shook his head, but he was moved by the raw kindness in his uncle's voice.

'Don't know yer dad well – but I've always been fond of yer mum. So is Prim, and she used to show it before she was took bad.'

'What's wrong with Auntie Prim?'

'She suffers from her nerves, lad. Runs in the family – like your mum.'

Desperate to change the subject for he didn't want to see any connection between his beloved mum and poor Auntie Prim, Andrew said: 'Why do the dogs go after badgers?'

'It's a sport – a good sport. Billy and I love it.'

'Isn't it cruel?'

'No, the badger puts up a good fight. Trouncer had an old boar by the short and curlies last weekend.'

'Don't the dogs get hurt?'

'They do. They've got battle scars all right.'

'But, but why do they do it?'

'I told you – the sport. And it gives 'em courage. They're working dogs, these terriers. Not just pretty faces. I mean working terrier shows aren't run by the Kennel Club.' He laughed, drawing on his pipe as the dogs played around him.

'Why not?' said Andrew.

'Well, they've got mixed ancestry for a start, so they can't be registered or recognised by the Kennel Club. My lot aren't judged on pedigree show points but on their aptitude for all the pursuits listed in the schedules. And one of these pursuits is going to ground after a badger. My five are worth quite a bit of money now.'

'Do you sell them, Uncle George?'

'Yes, lad. Breed 'em and sell 'em. They'll fetch up to fifty quid each when they've had a bit more experience.'

Andrew still felt the same iciness as he asked: 'Is badger digging allowed?'

Uncle George turned to him and winked. 'Not by law it isn't. But it doesn't stop us, I can tell you. Look, we're going digging tomorrow. It's Saturday and Billy will be home. You come with us – it's a great sport. Besides, we could use another spade.'

Before Andrew could reply Uncle George had turned and was beginning to walk uphill.

'Come on,' he said, whistling at the dogs, 'let's give 'em a run.'

They stood on a ridge overlooking the valley, both panting a little in the hard lunch-time sunlight.

'Of course, my Jenny hates me for it.' Uncle George sucked at his empty pipe, surveying the road below them, with its miniature cars and distant drone of noise. 'She – she's not been the same since her mum took queer. Not like my little girl any longer.'

Andrew wondered what he should say. He felt the note Jenny had written him, still lodged in his anorak pocket, and said nothing.

'She got in with a Gypsy bloke who took her badger watching and filled her head full of nonsense. I had to put a stop to it. I mean – he was old enough to be her father. Dirty old man, if you ask me. He's still lurking around somewhere. Still, I won't bother you with it. Before her mum took queer, and before the Gypo turned up, she was a smashing girl to her dad.'

Andrew sensed that Uncle George was very unhappy and felt sorry for him. But ever since he had started to talk about badger digging Andrew had been consumed by a cold anger. He thought of the badger in the copse the previous night and his anger hardened until it was like a painful coil deep inside his stomach that kept knotting until he could hardly breathe.

How could all this cruelty belong to the big gentle man his uncle had shown himself to be that morning? Did it have something to do with the way Auntie Prim was?

Throughout lunch, eaten in companionable silence with Uncle George, Andrew longed to explain Jenny's point of view. Questions tumbled about in his mind until his head ached.

'Now, lad, I've got to clean up the bar this afternoon,' Uncle George announced after lunch.

'Can I help?' asked Andrew dutifully, realising his opportunity had been missed.

'Go on, it's too good an afternoon for you to be cooped up indoors. You go out and explore. Billy'll be back at four and, being Friday, he won't have any homework. You can go out fishing again – but don't come back soaked this time.'

Uncle George went into the bar, booming with laughter, leaving Andrew thankfully to his own devices. He didn't know about the fishing later, but he did know where he was going now. He was going to find Brock.

6 Brock was difficult to find in the fierce heat of the June afternoon. Andrew's head ached as he climbed up the hill towards the wood, and the ground beneath his feet felt rock hard. The reddish soil sent up dust and the grazing cattle swished their tails miserably, trying to drive away the swarms of flies that besieged them. The sky above him was a deep blue and there were no clouds. Even the trees looked as if they were made of lead and the sun beat down with an intense, blinding glare. Andrew sweated as he walked in the white light and from the copse on the opposite side of the hill a jay made a single mocking call.

Brock's tent was deserted when Andrew reached the blessed relief of the cooler woodland. He sank down beside it, panting and desperately thirsty. For a moment he was tempted to look inside the tent to see if there was anything to drink, but decided he had better not. Andrew lay back on the ground and gradually his eyes began to close. He slept, dreaming of the Fulham streets and his dad's shop.

He saw his mother, looking much younger and fitter, sitting in an old chair on the sunlit street. His dad's truck drew up beside her and she jumped to her feet like a young girl and rushed forward to kiss him.

A gentle hand on his shoulder was gradually shaking Andrew awake. Startled and not quite sure where he was, he woke to find Brock bending over him.

His liquid eyes were kind, almost mischievous, as if they were already comrades in arms.

'And why am I privileged to have another visit?' he asked. For a moment Andrew felt unable to say anything. Then he stuttered:

'They've asked me to go badger digging.'

Brock frowned. 'Where?' Immediately he was tense but Andrew felt exhilarated. They were sharing something. It's us against the world, he thought.

'Right. I'll have the law on 'em.'

'Oh.' Andrew looked worried.

'It's all right. They'll only get a fine. No one's going to bang 'em up.'

'Now I feel a grass.'

'You are a grass – a super-grass.' Brock laughed. Once again, he had managed to frighten and reassure Andrew. It was extraordinary how compelling this made him.

'Fancy some lemonade?'

'You bet.'

'Some cold lemonade?'

'You got a fridge here?'

Brock laughed again. 'Not exactly.' He moved a few yards away and when he returned, to Andrew's amazement, he was holding a glistening bottle.

'Where's that come from?'

'There's a little spring down there. That's my fridge.'

He went to the tent, drew out two mugs and poured the lemonade into them. When Andrew sipped at his, it was deliciously cool.

'Good?'

'Mm.'

'Do you like living out here – in the open.'

'It's a bit dodgy in the winter but I usually get the use of a barn and snuggle up somewhere. Or I might get a bit of work and a farmer will put me up somewhere. I'm strong – a good worker.'

'But in summer – '

'I sleep rough. Under a hedgerow, in the woods – stars for a ceiling. It's great. You feel like an animal, curled up in the night.' He grinned at Andrew and ruffled his hair. 'You get to be tough though. When it rains I get wet. But you know, the strange thing is, I haven't caught a cold in years.'

They drank in silence for a while. Then Andrew said:

'I feel rotten shopping them. I quite like Uncle George.'

'He needs to be taught a lesson.' There was a sharp edge to Brock's voice.

'You won't mention that – '

'You told me? No, it'll just be a little surprise. When are they going?'

'Early tomorrow.'

'Right.'

There was silence again.

'Brock – '

'Yes.'

'Did you mind me coming up here?'

'I'm pleased. You've brought valuable information.'

'It's not fair on the badgers, is it?' said Andrew, seeking reassurance.

'No.'

'Why, why do they call you Brock?'

'*They* don't call me anything. It's Jenny's name for me.'

'What's your real name?'

'Ah, that would be telling.'

'Why do you live here? Is it because of the badgers?'

'I *do* like badgers, but it's not why I live here.'

'Then why?'

'To get some peace.'

Consumed by an insatiable curiosity Andrew was about to probe again when Brock said quietly:

'I was a teacher once.' His voice trailed away. 'And then some things happened – I lost someone.' Again his voice died. 'No more questions now.' He said in mock ferocity. 'I take people as they are. Here and now. Like you. I don't ask you where you've come from or where you're going to. Do I?'

'No.'

'Then there's no need to ask me. Is there?'

'No.'

'Have some more lemonade.'

Once again they sat in good, restful silence. Then Brock said, 'Tell you what, Andy – I like you. Don't you feel at peace out here?'

'Yes.'

'That's what my Jenny feels.' He looked round him. 'We're at one with everything here but only special people feel it – not everyone.'

'I'm special?'

'You don't disturb me,' said Brock. 'And you don't disturb nature. It's in your blood.'

Andrew had never felt so happy.

*

It was just as hot, walking down the hillside and past the baking cattle. The red mud was cracked under foot and there was a strong drone of traffic from a road he could not see. Feeling fresher after his rest Andrew started to climb halfway up the opposite hill towards the copse where the badgers lived. Eventually he reached it and, treading cautiously, went inside and walked slowly towards the sett. There was a great stillness, as if the whole wood was in suspended animation, waiting for the evening and the emergence of the badgers. Andrew tiptoed to one of the holes and sat down beside it, trying to imagine the badgers sleeping inside. Resting his chin on his knees, Andrew stared at the hole, other images – violent ones – replacing the peace of the present scene. He saw Uncle George and some equally big, rough men, armed with spades, surrounded by yapping terriers, determined to flush out the badgers. He could not have romantic images of defending Jenny and the badgers and defeating Uncle George for he saw he was up against overwhelming odds.

'I don't want to come.'
   'Why not?'
   'I just don't.'
   'But why not?'
   Silence.
   'It's good fun.'
   'Is it?'
   'Don't say you've been talking to Jenny.'
   Billy cast out his line, a look of contempt on his face.
   'She knows what she's talking about.'

'She's a *girl*.'

'So what?'

They were standing by the side of a wide stretch of shallow river that flowed under a low, stone bridge. It was evening and the temperature had dropped to a fading echo of the afternoon's heat. The water rippled translucently over rounded stones and Andrew cast his own line, his heart thumping with fear and renewed anger.

'She doesn't know what she's on about,' said Billy.

'She does. It's cruel.'

'Cruel? It's a sport, you moron.'

'You can play football, that's a sport. Digging up badgers is cruel.'

'It's training for the dogs.'

'Train them another way.'

'It's for the shows.'

'Don't go to the shows.'

'It's Dad's hobby.'

'Find another hobby.'

'You're a right twit, you are.'

'Get lost!'

'All right, I will. You can fish this bit – it's rotten anyway. I'll go upstream.'

Billy sulkily pushed past Andrew and set off up the narrow path beside the river. Left on his own, Andrew threw down his line and sat miserably on the bank. He desperately wanted to go home but he also wanted to stay on. He must fight for the badgers – and be near Jenny and Brock. Perhaps if Uncle George had a warning he wouldn't do it any more. Perhaps.

★

'Not coming, boy?'

'No thanks.'

'Why not?'

'He's been talking to Jenny.' Billy's voice was triumphant and Uncle George frowned over the cold supper he had prepared. Auntie Prim was still upstairs in her room but Jenny sat at the other end of the table, toying with her pork pie.

'Have you, lad?'

'I've given him my views,' said Jenny stolidly. 'But he's had to make up his own mind.'

Andrew spoke up. 'I don't see why you do it.'

'It's sport, lad and it's good for the dogs.'

'I think it's cruel.'

'Rubbish!' Uncle George downed some beer. 'Absolute bloody rubbish. And don't you say anything, Miss.'

'Andrew's a softie! Andrew's a softie!'

'You shut up – the lad's here on holiday. It's you who should be entertaining him. Why don't you take him to the swimming baths at Taunton tomorrow?'

Billy was immediately indignant. 'I want to come, Dad. You promised.'

'I'll take him in,' said Jenny.

Uncle George looked at her doubtfully. Then he turned to Andrew. 'Rather go with Billy, wouldn't you, son?'

'I don't mind going with Jenny.'

'I see.' Uncle George drained some more beer. Then he got up and fetched some fruit pies from the sideboard. 'Well, it's up to you.' He frowned again and Billy knew he was angry.

Andrew felt extremely uneasy and tried to

imagine how much angrier his uncle would be after he had been arrested tomorrow. It didn't bear thinking about.

That evening Andrew sat around watching television with Billy and Jenny whilst they all maintained a sulky silence. Eventually he went to bed early, saying a cursory good-night. Billy only grunted from his prone position on the floor, but Jenny looked up and smiled at him.

For what seemed like hours Andrew lay awake, as questions about tomorrow turned over in his mind. What would the police do to Uncle George and Billy, and anyone else, when they surprised them in Priory Wood? Jenny – or was it Brock? – had said they would only be fined, but suppose they were put in prison? He woke to the steel grey light of dawn creeping through the curtains and on to the bed. The light struck him with a chill that made his flesh creep. Then, about six o'clock, he fell into a deeper sleep and finally woke, exhausted and irritable. There was a knock on his door and he sat up in bed, expecting an aggressive Billy. Instead Jenny came in with a cup of tea. Andrew sighed aloud in relief.

'Hallo.'

'Brought you some tea.'

'Thanks.' He sipped it gratefully, suddenly realising how thirsty he was.

'You look tired.'

'Had a rotten night.'

'Thinking about today?'

'Yeah, I had a funny dream.'

'What dream?'

'I saw Brock sliding into a hole in the ground just like a badger. Then he came out again – and he was a badger.'

'You going off your nut?' asked Jenny.

Andrew sipped the tea again. 'I went to see Brock yesterday afternoon.' He glanced up at Jenny anxiously, wondering what her reaction would be.

'What!'

'I went to tell him that Uncle George and Billy are going badger digging this morning.'

'What did he say?'

'He said he'd tell the police – that it'd be a warning to him.'

'That means a change of plan for us,' said Jenny after a short pause. Andrew caught the note of resolution in her voice but only felt relief that she was not furious with him.

'To all intents and purposes we'll go swimming.'

'What's that supposed to mean?'

'It means we're going to double back to Priory Wood.'

'But – '

'And hide.'

'Isn't that a bit mean?' Andrew already felt bad at having shopped his uncle and Billy and intensely disliked the idea of watching them being arrested.

'Mean!' Jenny looked angry. 'Why should it be mean?'

Andrew finished off his tea and tried another tack. 'They'll see us.'

'No they won't. I've got a safe place to hide. No one will ever find us.'

'You sure?'

'I've hidden there before.'

'And watched them?'

'Yes. Well, are you coming?'

Andrew was silent.

'I must see them being taught a lesson.' Jenny insisted.

'Oh, all right then.'

Andrew put down his cup. Providing he was near Jenny nothing else really seemed to matter.

7 'I'm puffed.'

'Hurry up.'

They were stumbling over the uneven ground that led off the main road. The overgrown path climbed steeply upwards to a hill that overlooked Priory Wood. It was as hot as yesterday – if not hotter – and they were sweating as they carried their bathing costumes and towels under their arms.

'I wish we *had* gone for a swim now,' said Andrew guiltily, but Jenny firmly urged him on until they came to the crest of the hill, flopping down in the long grass exhausted.

'Here we are.'

Below them was a dense clump of trees that stretched for a square mile or so. Nothing moved. It was eleven in the morning and the sun was riding high in another cloudless sky.

'I don't see anyone.'

'They'll be here soon.'

Andrew chewed at a grass stalk, half expecting to

see lines of policemen hidden somewhere on the outskirts of the wood.

'We won't see anything from here.'

'But we will from over there. Come on.'

She jumped to her feet and Andrew staggered to his. Jenny had all the energy of purpose, but he was beginning to be part of it. It was a far cry from his waking dreams of defending Jenny and the badgers from the marauding hunters.

They walked along the ridge and to Andrew's dismay then began to descend towards Priory Wood.

'They'll see us.'

'They're not here yet.'

They arrived on the outskirts of the thick woodland and began to walk towards its core.

'Supposing they see us.'

'Hurry up.'

Eventually they reached a huge, ivy-shrouded oak tree that stood towering above the rest of the wood.

'Can you climb?'

'Yes.'

'Then climb.'

Jenny levered herself into the dense mass of the branches and Andrew followed her as quickly as he could. The ivy was dusty and slippery to the feet, but the branches were like a natural step-ladder and soon they were high above, out of sight.

'Now look down,' whispered Jenny.

Andrew did as he was told, feeling a moment's dizziness.

'Blimey.'

He could see a glade to the right and in one corner there was a large badger sett.

'Now shush.'

'What do we do?'

'What do you think? Sing hymns? Shut up and wait.'

They both jammed themselves into the junction of two great branches and settled down to wait.

They did not have to wait long. Jenny and Andrew stiffened as they heard the sound of barking. Slowly they came into view – three big men followed by the even bigger Uncle George, who carried a bag, and the diminutive Billy. They had spades over their shoulders and each held a terrier on a short lead. The dogs were furiously excited and the men were jocular, animated.

For a while nothing happened and Jenny and Andrew relaxed slightly in their tree as beer was produced, pipes and cigarettes lit and jokes were exchanged. Andrew could see that Billy was drinking coke and his already dry throat felt parched with thirst. He thought of Brock's cool lemonade of yesterday and swallowed with difficulty. Meanwhile the terriers panted in the shade, their eyes never moving from the area around the sett.

'Time to get started then,' said Uncle George at length, getting to his feet. The men rose more reluctantly, stretching and yawning, whilst Billy swilled back the last of his coke. From the bag Uncle George drew a sack and a strange-looking instrument that to Andrew appeared to resemble a pair of tongs. It had wooden handles and an iron head with blunt teeth. Andrew felt a cold sweat break out on his forehead as he stared down at the fearsome device.

Uncle George took a terrier towards one of the entrances to the sett and nuzzled him at it. For a few seconds the terrier stood still, growling, whilst the others strained at their leashes, setting up a cacophony of yapping and barking. Then the terrier, hackles rising, darted down the tunnel. For a while nothing happened, and the men stood tensely at the entrance. Billy gathered up the spades and placed them near to hand. There was complete silence in the glade and Andrew found that he could hardly breathe. A short, sharp bark suddenly broke the stillness but the four terriers remained tensely silent. Clearly the warning bark had come from below ground. After a few seconds there were more barks and Andrew had the feeling that they came from a different part of the sett. As more excited barks emerged, Andrew knew that a deadly chase was now actually taking place beneath the red earth.

Uncle George was bending over the sett, listening intently to the sound of the barking terrier. Suddenly he turned to the others and Andrew heard him say:

'O.K. lads, the badger's taken up his position and he's gonna face it out. Let's get digging.'

At once they all began digging furiously and Uncle George produced a couple of picks from his bag to make the going easier. Grunting, sweating and cursing, the four men and Billy worked as hard as they could, whilst the dogs squatted beside them, silent and obedient. Still the shrill barks emerged as the digging continued. They were cutting off the badgers' means of retreat and Andrew's anger intensified.

Suddenly the terrier below ground gave a terrible

yelp followed by an agonised yowling that was piteous to hear.

Jenny whispered: 'He's got him, oh yes, he's got him. Well done!'

'What do you mean?' he hissed at her.

'The badger's savaged him and serve him damn well right!' she crowed. 'Look at Dad.'

Uncle George had stopped digging and was crouched anxiously at the mouth of the sett yelling:

'Trouncer, Trouncer, come here, boy.'

But the terrible yowling continued and Andrew winced as he heard the pain.

'Trouncer! Come *on*, boy.'

Still the yowling went on, piteous in its intensity.

'Here, boy. Here. Trouncer!'

Suddenly there was silence, followed by a plaintive whimpering. Uncle George continued to call and the others crouched round the sett, too, all looking distraught.

'Trouncer. Here, boy. It's – all – right – boy. Out you come, boy.'

But still the terrier did not emerge from the sett and Andrew began to feel sick.

The whimpering continued but now it seemed to be nearer to the hole where the terrier had entered and Uncle George crouched even closer to it, his arms outstreched and his face working with emotion. Andrew was beginning to feel extremely sorry for Billy when Jenny nudged him so sharply that he almost fell out of the tree.

'Look!'

The terrier was painfully emerging from the hole. It was covered in blood.

*

Five minutes later George Lammas had tied up the ear that was flapping loose over the terrier's head and had also strapped up the deeply gouged leg. Trouncer was quieter now, but Andrew could see his whole body shivering on the soft floor of the glade.

'Will he be all right, Dad?' said Billy anxiously.

'I think so, son. He's lost a lot of blood, that's the rub.'

'We'll have to carry him home,' said one of the men.

'Another day's sport over, eh?' said another.

Uncle George shrugged. 'Vicious bloody brute.'

'It's an old sett,' said one of the men. 'Bloody maze down there.'

'Tell you what,' said the third man. 'There's a newer sett over at Tench – in a copse. Haven't seen it but Sam Hart told me about it.'

Andrew felt Jenny stiffen. 'It's our copse,' she whispered.

'Oh, no.'

'And they've been bloodied.'

Her voice was high with anxiety and Andrew's fear intensified. Meanwhile, in the glade Uncle George lovingly and gently scooped Trouncer into his arms and began to walk off. The others followed, a slow-moving party, dour and silent. The dogs trotted along with them, equally subdued. The last to leave the glade was Billy, who was struggling with the bag and his spade. As he disappeared into the trees Andrew whispered:

'What happened to the police?'

Jenny and Andrew soon found out what the police

66

had been doing. They had arrested Brock. The news came out over a late lunch, which was a miserable affair of stale pork pie and boiled potatoes. They had commiserated over Trouncer, who had returned from the vet with stitches in his ear and leg. Although he had lost a lot of blood, the vet had assured a relieved Uncle George that all would be well.

'We'll get that badger,' said Billy threateningly.

'Don't be so childish, it was defending itself,' said Jenny. 'What else could the poor thing do?'

'All right, all right,' said Uncle George. 'Don't you two start. Enjoy your swim, Andy?'

'It was great,' he replied. They had dampened their swimming things in a pond but Andrew had been worried that they did not smell of chlorine.

Then Billy burst out:

'Guess what we found out at the vet?'

'What?' said Jenny sounding exhausted.

'That Gypo. He got nicked.'

'Gypo?'

'The one who fancied you.'

'Billy – that's enough!' said Uncle George.

Jenny was immediately afraid and Andrew could see that she was struggling to control her feelings. He wanted desperately to help her, but he didn't know how.

'What Gypo?' she repeated nervously.

'They told us at the vet. He's the bloke all right. They arrested him,' said Uncle George.

'What for?' asked Jenny.

Andrew had to admire Jenny's icy self-control.

'They've been after him for a long time – he's been on the run. Fraud or something. Apparently he's been living out in Cloud Copse near Tench – doing odd jobs for old Parker. Got a tent – the lot.'

'Cloud Copse is where our next dig is gonna be,' said Billy maliciously, studying Jenny's expression. But she still gave nothing away and Andrew hated Billy for his insensitivity.

'What will happen to the Gypo?' asked Andrew.

'He'll be taken before the Bench tomorrow,' said Uncle George. 'Over in Taunton.'

Jenny got up. 'I've had enough,' she said.

'There's apple pies to follow,' said her father gently.

'No thanks.' She hurried to the door, just a shade too quickly.

When Jenny had gone, Andrew, surprised at his own calm duplicity, said:

'Who is he?'

'No one knows. Middle-aged bloke who set his cap at my Jenny – said he was interested in natural history. Soon sorted him out.'

Uncle George lumbered to his feet, taking out the dishes. When he had gone Billy said:

'He's a dirty old man, that Gypo.'

'How do you know?'

'I just know.'

Andrew stared at him with hostility and Billy grinned, pleased that he had antagonised him.

'You fancy Jenny too, don't you?'

Andrew rose to his feet, his fists clenched. 'Shut up!'

'It's all right if you fancy her – I don't mind.'

'I said – shut up.'

'Andy fancies Jenny! Andy fancies – '

Andrew could take no more. He threw himself at

Billy, knocking him off his chair. They rolled to the ground, punching and kicking at each other. As they fought, Uncle George came back with the apple pies. Dumping them down on the table, he stood over Billy and Andrew for a moment. Then he bent down, grabbed them both and separated them as if they were terriers.

'What the hell are you two on about?'

'Nothing,' said Andrew, but the panting Billy was more truthful.

'It was my fault, Dad.'

'Oh?'

'I said he fancied Jenny.'

Uncle George chortled. 'Well he's a bit young but why not? My Jenny's a lovely girl.' Then he grew more serious. 'Now look, you two, why don't you stop scrappin' and try to get on with each other. What are you going to do this afternoon?'

'Don't know,' said Andrew.

'Tell you what,' said Billy, 'I'll show him Imman's Lake – we could swim there.' He turned to Andrew. 'If you can take another swim?' He grinned but the grin was no longer challenging. In fact it was almost friendly.

'What do you say, Andy?' asked Uncle George.

'I don't mind.'

'O.K.,' said Billy. 'I'll feed the dogs, take a look at Trouncer and meet you round the front.'

'And mind – no more scrappin',' said Uncle George.

8 Andrew crept quickly up to Jenny's bedroom and knocked on the door.

'Who is it?' Her voice was muffled and tearful.

'Me.'

'You can't come in.'

'Are you all right?'

'What do you think?'

'What shall we do without Brock?'

'I don't know.'

'Supposing they go to our copse?'

'They will.'

Andrew's voice broke. 'I can't bear it – can you?'

There was silence. Then she said: 'I'm not going to.'

'What do you mean?'

'If Brock can't do anything – I'm going to. *I'm* going to call the police.'

'Blimey!'

'I don't care if they *are* my own family. Besides – '

'Besides what?'

'Oh – nothing.'

'Do you really think that Brock did something wrong?'

'No – ' her voice was fierce – 'of course he didn't.'

'What are you going to do?'

'I'm off to the police. This afternoon.'

'Blimey!'

'Don't keep saying that.'

'What are you going to tell them?'

'About the digging – and about Brock.'

'What will you say?'

'Listen, stupid – it's quite simple. I'll tell them to trap Dad when he tries to trap the badgers. I'm also going to tell them Brock didn't do anything.'

'Will they listen to you?'

'I'll make them – now go away.' Jenny's voice was authoritative and Andrew crept obediently away, feeling utterly useless.

Andrew could hardly bear the strain of going to Imman's Lake with Billy, but there was no way of getting out of it. The lake was a strange, sinister place set up high in the hills. They walked a long way, mainly in silence, but the heat was not quite as intense so the going was made a little easier. When they arrived at the lake they both flopped down on a kind of grassy sandy shore that stretched beside it. The water looked murky and uninviting and the sun was now hidden by a dull grey cloud cover. There were rank-looking weeds at one end of the lake and a muddy foreshore over which some midges swarmed.

'It's smashing when you get in,' said Billy, putting on his trunks. He seemed to want to be friendly now but Andrew was not so willing.

'Doesn't look like it.'

He sat in his jeans and tee-shirt, loath to change.

'Come on, Andy. Please.'

Reluctantly Andrew changed and they both walked a little hesitantly into the water. But it *was* smashing and Andrew was very surprised at the soft coolness of the dull water. After splashing around for a while and ducking each other, they both swam lazily to the centre and lay on their backs, gazing up at the sky. Then Andrew turned over again and began to swim slowly to the opposite side. He heard Billy shout something but he could not make out what it was. Diving beneath the surface, Andrew felt himself being brushed by something soft and spongy. It was like being in the dark in a ghost train when the strands of cobwebs touched your face. Opening his eyes Andrew saw that he was swimming through a dense jungle of sinewy, translucent weeds. They had an underwater life of their own, moving in a soft bubbling harmony that utterly repelled Andrew. With a backward kick, he tried to shoot up to the surface, only to find his ankle firmly entangled in a mass of weed.

For seconds which seemed like hours, Andrew struggled in his trap in rising panic. He managed to break the surface with one of his arms, but the more he struggled with his foot, the tighter the grip of the weeds became. Just as he thought he could hold out no longer, he saw Billy diving down beside him. He seemed to know exactly what to do as he cleaved down to the weeds. Suddenly Andrew felt a glorious sense of release as his foot was freed and he shot gasping to the surface. Billy surfaced beside him, putting an arm round his shoulders.

'Are you O.K.?'

'Yeah,' Andrew gasped.

'Can you make it back to the shore?'

'I – I think so.' His breath was coming in great sobs.

'Sure?'

'I'll try.'

Slowly Andrew swam back to the muddy shore while Billy kept close beside him. They both staggered out and lay on the ground.

'Thanks,' said Andrew eventually, when his breathing was easier.

'O.K. now?' asked Billy anxiously.

'Could have been nasty.'

'I shouted to you not to go up there. It's the dangerous end.'

'I didn't hear.'

'I should have told you before we went in.' Billy sounded unusually contrite.

'It's not your fault.' Andrew sat up slowly. 'Do you know – you saved my life.'

'Rubbish.'

'But you did. How did you know what to do?'

'Because I got stuck once – and Jen rescued me.'

'Oh.'

'I'm sorry about what I said.' Billy's sudden apology made Andrew start.

'What?'

''Bout you and Jen.'

'Oh.'

'I was angry – about Trouncer.'

'He's going to be all right, isn't he?'

'Yeah, I think so.'

'Look – ' Andrew hesitated. 'Do you think this badger digging is right?'

'It's a sport, isn't it? Besides Jen only doesn't like it 'cos of her old Gypo.'

'That's not true.'

'She was right fond of him.'

Gradually, Andrew was feeling more and more uneasy as he kept thinking about Jenny at the police station. He longed to tell Billy what was in store for him tomorrow. He should at least warn him. But then, with a feeling of sick despair, Andrew realised that he couldn't warn Billy even if he had just saved his life.

'What's up?' asked Billy and Andrew started, worried that he might have given something away by the expression on his face.

'Nothing,' he replied hastily.

'You O.K.? Not swallowed too much water. Hey, you're shivering.'

Andrew *was* shivering but he couldn't work out whether it was because he had nearly drowned or because he felt really guilty. Then Billy made it worse.

'You know what,' he said.

'What?'

'We could be mates – even if you don't like badger digging.'

'Yeah – we – we could be.'

'Shall we?'

'Be mates? Yeah – we could be.'

'All right then,' said Billy, 'we are.'

9 Over tea Jenny said there was a disco on in Taunton.

'Can we go, Dad?' asked Billy. They had agreed

not to mention the water incident for reasons they could not fathom. It seemed like a bond between them that not even Jenny could share.

'All right,' said Uncle George. 'I'll run you in. Both you lads going?'

'You bet,' said Billy and Andrew in unison.

'It's a junior disco at the youth club, is it?' he asked Jenny. 'Because if it's anything else – '

'No,' said Jenny quickly. 'It's nothing else.' She seemed very strained and Andrew wondered what had happened between her and the police.

'O.K.,' said Uncle George. 'I'll run you in at seven – and pick you up at eleven.'

'What about the bar, Dad?' asked Billy.

'I've got Ernie coming in. It'll be O.K.'

'What about Mum?'

'Gladys will do for her. She's not herself.'

'Where is she?' asked Jenny with a dead note in her voice.

'Upstairs,' replied her father. 'She's not herself again.'

'Who's not herself?' The voice was slurred and raucous. Auntie Prim was in their midst, staggering and looking more than ever like a sad, painted clown.

Andrew glanced at Uncle George and saw the tender pain on his face.

'Come on now, Prim,' he said, moving towards her. 'You should be upstairs.'

'Why? Are you ashamed of me or something?'

'Come on, old girl.'

'Don't you "old girl" me!'

Uncle George attempted to put an arm round her waist but she pushed him away and staggered back.

'Don't you come near me, you bastard!'

Andrew felt a sense of shock as she spat out the words.

'Now look – ' Uncle George paused indecisively.

'You ashamed of me or something?' she said again, voicing everyone's thoughts.

'You're not well. Let me take you upstairs.' Uncle George put his arm round her waist for the second time, but much more resolutely than he had before. He began to steer her towards the door although Auntie Prim, struggling furiously, tried to resist him. It was an unpleasant sight as she pushed against the vastly superior strength of her husband while he half-carried her towards the door.

'Damn you,' she said. 'Damn you.' Her voice was thick and the odour of gin was now much stronger than her customarily overpowering scent of violets.

'For God's sake, Mum, go up to bed. You're not fit to be seen!' Jenny shouted.

At this Auntie Prim's face crumpled as if she had received a mortal blow. She allowed herself to be dragged out of the room and all three of them listened as Uncle George slammed the kitchen door. There was the sound of a blow and then a cry of pain.

'No, Dad!' screamed Jenny and threw herself at the door. But small though he was Billy grabbed his sister by the arm and held her gently but firmly.

'Don't you interfere,' he said.

'He's hurting her,' she sobbed. Then she seemed to compose herself and turned with tearful dignity to Andrew. 'My mother's not too well tonight. She's having one of her turns.'

★

They were a silent and subdued group as Uncle George ran them into Taunton. He tried to make conversation, booming on about matters of local interest, but he only received monosyllabic answers and soon gave up. He left them in an old church hall that had been transformed into a thundering, grinding, glaring disco. The noise was so tremendous that they did not have to speak. Billy joined a group of friends, leaving Jenny and Andrew alone. For a while they gyrated to the music but after ten minutes Jenny touched Andrew's arm and yelled in his ear:

'Let's go outside.'

They wandered down the quiet street, not feeling the need to talk. They came to a low wall. It was dark and cool shadows were creeping over the baked stonework.

'Badgers will be out,' said Andrew.

'Mm.'

'How – how did you get on with the police?'

'I didn't.' Her voice was low and bitter.

'What do you mean?'

'The desk sergeant didn't think I should tell on my dad. He seemed to think it was pretty rotten. Besides, he said there wasn't much he could do.'

'But it's illegal.'

'Yes, and if he caught Dad at it he'd be for the high jump.'

'Well, he can if he keeps watch on the copse.'

'He said he couldn't spare the men to keep surveillance on badgers.'

'So how *will* they be stopped?'

'They won't.'

Andrew looked away.

'He said the police are better off catching villains. And did I think my dad was a villain?'

'So they won't help.'

'No.'

'Supposing your dad catches a boar and sets it against the terriers in your back yard?'

'I didn't get as far as that.'

'Why not?'

'He made me feel ashamed. He made me feel ashamed of trying to – get my dad arrested.'

'Then what about the badgers? How can we protect them? I'm sure your dad will go to the copse.' Suddenly Andrew was very angry.

'There's only one thing I can do.'

'What?'

'Take a non-violent civil action.'

'Eh?'

'I'm going to lie across the sett until they go away. And if they want to send the terriers in, then they'll have to go over me.'

'That's no good.'

'Why not?'

'They'll pick you up and drag you away.'

'I'll fight.'

'Then it won't be non-violent.'

She shook her head disconsolately. 'It's the only thing I can do.'

'That *we* can do.'

'You mean – '

'Well, you're not doing it alone.' Andrew spoke firmly and without any sign of doubt in his voice.

'Thanks,' Jenny said simply. Andrew's spirits soared.

★

Half an hour later Andrew and Jenny walked back to the hall and went to buy a coke. Andrew felt closer than he had ever been to Jenny and was sure that she felt the same. As they drank their cokes Jenny kept giving Andrew cautious looks, as if she was wondering whether she could fully trust him. Then she spoke hurriedly, almost willing herself to take a risk.

'You know my father sleeps around?'

'You mean he sleeps with other women?'

'He has for years. Mum – couldn't take it.'

'I'm sorry.'

'There's nothing anyone can do now. She's been to hospital. Twice.'

'Does he still?'

'Not so much now. He – he's sorry. Sorry about what he did and sorry for her. But it's too late.'

There was a pause then Andrew asked:

'Why does he dig up badgers?'

'He's always done it. It's part of him – there's something in him that wants to destroy.'

'Why?'

'I don't know.'

'You hate him, don't you?'

Jenny turned on him with a kind of fierce pity. 'Of course I don't really hate him. I love him. He's my dad.'

'But you said – ' Andrew felt a fool now, for he realised he had misjudged a very important part of Jenny's complicated personality.

'I keep saying I hate him. Of course I hate him. But I love him too.'

'Yes.' Andrew stared at the ground, not understanding her, almost frightened by her vehemence. 'What about Billy?'

'Oh, he's like Dad. He follows him.' Jenny suddenly jumped to her feet. 'Come on, let's dance,' she said.

Andrew reluctantly went with her.

Ten minutes later, Andrew made an excuse and slipped out again into the summer night, this time on his own. He wanted to think. It was true that what was happening to the badgers seemed monstrously cruel, but Uncle George and Billy weren't monsters. They might be a bit rough, but if they came to Fulham – well, they'd fit in well enough. Then there was Brock. Andrew's head pounded and for a moment all he could see was Brock, standing in the clearing of Cloud Copse. He seemed to be part of the trees and the landscape and the badgers and Jenny. The pounding in his head gradually stopped and Andrew realised how jealous of Brock he was.

On the way home Jenny decided that she was going to launch a verbal attack on her father in the car.

'Dad?'

'Yes. Did you have a good time?'

'Great,' said Billy who obviously had.

'It was all right,' said Jenny.

'And you, Andy.'

'It was fine, Uncle George.'

'So it was only Lady Muck who didn't enjoy herself?' There was a challenge in his voice and at once Andrew felt the tension in the atmosphere. He suspected his uncle had been drinking.

'I told you – it was all right.'

'Not good enough for you, eh?'

'I don't want to talk about it, Dad.'

'No?'

'I want to talk about something else.'

'What?'

'Badgers.'

'Oh no, we've had enough of that.'

Andrew's heart plunged. Surely she must realise that she had chosen absolutely the wrong time to bring up the subject.

'No, we haven't, Dad.'

'Look I'm tired, love.'

'Are you going to dig in that copse?'

'You bet I am,' said Uncle George aggressively.

'Then I'm going to stop you.'

'Don't be damn silly.'

'I'm not going to allow you to do it.'

'In fact, I'm going to dig the whole copse up!'

'It's not to do with badgers, Dad, is it? It's to do with him.'

'Shut up!'

'It's true, isn't it? You're getting at him, aren't you? That's all – you're against him and her and me.'

'Shut up – or I'll stop this car and give you the damn good hiding you deserve.'

Strangely, unexpectedly, Jenny quietened. She was sitting in front and Andrew could see that her shoulders were shaking.

'Now,' said Uncle George in an attempt to regain normality, 'what bits of stuff did you lads get off with then?'

Andrew was wondering what on earth Jenny had

meant that night. Her words rang in his ears until the early hours of the morning.

Just as Andrew had finally fallen into a deep sleep, he was abruptly awakened by the sound of sobbing. Looking at his watch he saw it was 3 a.m. The sobbing was very loud, low-pitched, almost gutteral, and came from directly outside his door. For a couple of minutes Andrew froze, terrified at the animal-sound. Then the note changed to a kind of wailing and Andrew was deeply relieved to hear the sound of Uncle George's voice, albeit hoarse and angry.

'What the hell are you doing, woman?'

'She's gone to him.'

'What!'

'She's gone to him. Her room's empty.'

'Bloody hell!'

Andrew now recognised Auntie Prim's voice. Then he heard his uncle thundering off in the direction of Jenny's room. There was a crash as the door was flung open, a silence and then a fierce shout:

'Where the bloody hell is she?'

'She's – '

'Oh shut up, woman!'

'What's the matter, Dad?' Andrew heard Billy's voice, fearful and still full of sleep.

'It's your sister. She's not in her room.'

'Where is she?'

'God knows.'

'You said he was out, George.'

'Who?' Billy's voice was shrill with fear.

'Nobody.'

But Auntie Prim was determined to have her say and her voice rose stridently.

'*He's* out.'

'Who's out, Mum?'

'One more word and I'll knock your block off,' snarled Uncle George. 'Stay in your room, Billy. I'm going to phone the police.'

Andrew lay still in bed, deciding to pretend he was asleep, whilst Billy questioned his mother on the landing.

'Who's out, Mum?'

'Her – ' She paused as if changing her mind about something. 'The badger man. He's out.'

'But he was in prison.'

'He was at the police station. He got away – and a policeman's injured.'

'How?'

'*I* don't know, son. They were out in the village after closing time looking for him and – '

There was a roar of anger as Uncle George rejoined them. He was out of breath and there was something in his voice that Andrew could not at first discern. With a shock he realised that it was fear.

'I told you to go to bed, Billy.'

'Sorry, Dad.'

'Go!'

Andrew heard the sound of Billy's scurrying feet. Then Uncle George said to Auntie Prim:

'Go back to bed!'

'How can I when I know he's out?' To Andrew's surprise, she sounded almost normal – just a very frightened person.

'Look, the police are out in force.'

'Where are they looking, George?'

'Here, where he used to be.'

'That copse?'

'Yeah, now – '

'There's something else, isn't there? What else aren't you telling me George?'

'Nothing.'

'Come on, George. What is it?'

Reluctantly he said: 'Jenny was down at the nick yesterday afternoon.'

'Why?'

'Some cock and bull story about me digging.'

'That's no cock and bull story.'

'Tried to get me nicked. My own daughter!'

'She was right. She knows why you do it.'

'Rubbish!'

'To get at him.'

'You're crazy, woman.'

'It's you – eaten up with jealousy.'

'He's got no right to her. She's mine.'

'He's got every right – and she knows it.'

'He's no more than a vagrant – a cheap little crook. Can't even hold down a job without dipping his fingers . . .'

'I didn't know that when he came.'

'Living in a tent in a wood. What kind of – '

Then Andrew heard Billy's voice again. 'Dad – '

'I told you to – '

'She's back.'

'What?'

'She came up the back stairs.'

'Jenny!'

'She's back in her room.'

'Jenny!'

'You hurt a hair of that girl's head, George – '

'Shut up, woman.'

'I'll have the law on you.'

'Jenny!'

'Don't hurt her, Dad, please,' Billy pleaded.

'Jenny!'

'Yes?'

Andrew lay in bed shivering. Then he heard Jenny's voice on the landing, saying something to Billy.

'Where the hell have you been?' demanded Uncle George.

'I went for a walk.'

'At *this* time of night?'

'I couldn't sleep.'

'Pull the other one.'

'It's true, Dad.'

'You little liar!' Andrew jerked up in bed as he heard Uncle George strike her. There was a cry of pain and then Jenny said in a very high, tremulous voice:

'It's true, Dad.'

'You've been with him, haven't you?'

'Are you barmy?'

'Don't touch her again, George,' Auntie Prim screamed.

'Dad, leave her!' Billy's voice was very shrill and sounded as if he had been crying.

'Hit me if you want – if it makes you feel better,' Jenny taunted.

'You've been with him – admit it.'

'No!'

'All right. I'm not going to touch you. I wouldn't soil my hands.'

'Do you think Andy is sleeping through all this, Dad?' asked Billy.

'I don't give a damn what he's doing,' said Uncle George.

'You want him to know all our private business?' Jenny asked.

'He probably knows it all – I expect you told him.'

'I didn't tell him – about that.'

'You surprise me. So you expect me to believe you've been for a walk at three in the morning – when he's on the loose?'

'What do you mean?'

'He did a bunk, they're looking for him.'

'I didn't know that.'

'They've searched the copse.'

Unexpectedly there was total silence. Then Uncle George said:

'I gather you tried to get me nicked?'

'What?'

'Don't try and protest. The police were round here at midnight – looking for him. They told me then that you'd asked after him. And on the phone just now they said how you'd tried to get me nicked.'

'So I did.'

'But they weren't interested in nicking yer dad, were they?'

'They should have been.'

'How could you, Jen?' The fear in Billy's voice had gone, to be replaced by an anger that was similar to his father's.

'I could,' she replied.

'Why?'

'He shouldn't do it. He should leave them alone.'

'Why don't you, George? That would solve one problem.' Auntie Prim's voice was steady and controlled.

'Shut up!'

'Don't speak to Mum like that,' said Jenny quietly.

'Listen, my fine lady, don't tell me what to do. Remember this – I'll dig up those badgers any time I like – and I'll run that Gypo to earth if I can.'

'It's one and the same, isn't it?' said Auntie Prim and Andrew heard Uncle George give another roar of anger. He was obviously advancing on her and Andrew jumped out of bed and ran to the door. When he opened it he saw Uncle George standing with his great fist upraised a few inches from Auntie Prim who had pushed herself up against the banisters. Jenny and Billy were desperately holding on to him and they all froze when Andrew appeared.

'What's the matter?' he asked.

Part Two **Gone To Earth**

1 'He's in the outhouse,' whispered Jenny to Andrew when they were alone the next morning.

'Who?'

'Brock.'

'What?' Andrew's mind reeled with the shock of events that seemed rapidly to be getting out of control.

'I said – he's in the outhouse.'

Andrew stared at Jenny as if she were quite mad. They were standing in the yard, surrounded by the barking terriers, ostensibly feeding them.

'But the dogs – '

'It's right round the other side of the house. There's an allotment down there and this old shed at the bottom.'

'But it's the first place they'll look!' Andrew realised that the only reason Jenny was so cool was because she was desperate and he knew it was up to him to help her, however dangerous the situation had become.

'It's the most obvious. So they won't look there, will they?'

'You're crazy!'

'Yes. I probably am.'

'He's a criminal.'

'Is he? He's not been tried yet.'

'But to escape – '

'Oh, they'd have found him guilty.'

'Why?'

'Because of the way he looks.'

Then something else occurred to Andrew – it had been nagging at him for some time.

'Look, I don't understand what you meant in the car last night when . . .'

But she quickly interrupted him. 'Are you going to help me?'

'Help you? What with?'

'His escape. Well?' Jenny looked at him challengingly.

'As a matter of fact – ' began Andrew.

'Yes?' He could see the disappointment on her face and a flash of desperation for he knew she was thinking that he was going to refuse. Andrew had never seen her like this before and he suddenly felt on a much more equal level with her.

'I'll help you.'

Instantly she flung her arms round his neck and kissed him on the forehead. 'I knew you'd help.'

'But tell me something.'

'What?' She withdrew and he could see the suspicion in her eyes.

'Why is he so important to you?'

'I told you – because everybody – '

'Jenny – *why*?'

She looked at him in silence. 'If I tell you,' she said slowly, 'you must promise never to tell anyone else.'

'I promise.'

'He's my father,' she said.

★

'I'm going to take the jumble up in Johnson's cart,' said Jenny.

Uncle George nodded. He seemed to have lost some of his spirit overnight and he sat before the Sunday morning breakfast table, slumped into his newspaper, his pipe empty and a cup of stewed dark tea at his elbow.

'You mind that horse on the roads.'

'You know I've done it before. Dozens of times. I can – '

'O.K. O.K. Off you go.' He turned away, sipping at the brackish tea.

Auntie Prim and Billy were still upstairs as Jenny and Andrew left the room. Andrew's mind was still reeling from what Jenny had told him. Brock. Her father? It didn't make sense. But she gave him no time to question her further for directly they were outside the house, she turned on him urgently.

'Just do as I say. We've got to move fast.'

'O.K.'

'I'm going down the road to borrow the horse and cart. Just in front of the allotment there's a pile of old blankets and junk under a big tarpaulin. Start moving it all back to the gate by the shed.'

'I didn't see a gate,' said Andrew hesitantly.

'Well, there is one, stupid. A small gate out on to the road. Leave the blankets till last. Do you understand?'

'How long are you going to be?'

'About a quarter of an hour.'

'What happens if anyone comes out? Billy, for instance.'

'Get him to help you. Don't act suspicious – whatever you do. And don't go near the shed.'

Without waiting for further comment, Jenny hurried off down the road. When she had gone, Andrew realised that he had never felt so alone in his life.

The minutes passed like hours and Andrew felt more and more nervous. He kept looking towards The Packhorse but there were no signs of life. Five minutes passed while he hauled the jumble through the gate and on to the road. Seven minutes, eight, nine! The sun was as intense as ever and Andrew was soon covered with a drenching sweat that continuously ran into his eyes. Nine and a half –

'Andy!'

Andrew turned, his stomach heaving. It was Billy, looking tousled and sleepy.

'What are you doing?'

'Jenny said to help with the jumble.'

'It's not till this afternoon.'

'She said to help.'

'Where is she?'

'Gone to fetch the horse and cart.'

'What the hell for? We always take it in the truck.'

'I think she likes driving the cart.'

'She would.'

He seemed out of sorts and suspicious, his eyes moving over the piles of books and old toys, pictures and clothes and old blankets as if – as if what? Andrew wondered if he suspected anything and he thought of Brock, crouched in the shed, so near.

'Want some help?'

'I can manage.'

'Be like that.'

'Sorry – if you want to help – '

'O.K.'

Billy started to pick up a box of books, but just as he was doing so, Andrew heard the sound of hooves and the rattle of the cart. She was early. Thank God she was early.

Both boys went through the gate and watched her pull up a large chestnut horse and a small, rather dilapidated-looking cart.

'You'll never get it all in there. Why don't we use the truck as well?'

Andrew almost screamed aloud but Jenny seemed to be quite calm and confident.

'No thanks. I like driving the cart.'

'Dad won't mind.'

'I want him to rest.' She gave Billy a warning look. 'After last night – you know.'

'Yeah.'

'O.K. Let's load up. Junk first, blankets last. Then bung the tarpaulin over everything.'

'You don't want the – '

'Billy, just do as I say. I'm tired.'

'O.K. O.K.'

Grudgingly Billy began to help them. As he worked Andrew admired Jenny's handling of her brother. She'd make a good con-woman, he thought. She was so utterly convincing.

When the cart was full, Billy grabbed one end of the tarpaulin and gave it a yank. 'No rope,' he said.

'Get some from the house,' she yelled from the top of the cart and Andrew's stomach churned again. This was the moment. Then Billy said:

'There's some in the shed.'

The words seemed to fall over them like drops of icy water and Andrew shivered in the heat.

'I put it in the house last night. Back of the kitchen cabinet.'

'What the hell for?'

'Didn't think it looked safe. I was going to take a closer look at it – only I didn't have time. Can you get it?'

'What do *you* know about rope?'

'What do *you*?' she retorted. 'Now are you going to get it or not?'

'All right.' Protesting vigorously, Billy walked off at a snail's pace in the direction of the house. When he was out of sight, Jenny leapt from the top of the cart to the ground and rushed into the shed. In a few seconds Brock emerged, looked round him frantically and then flung himself into the cart. He buried himself into the junk and the blankets with what seemed an appalling amount of noise.

'Quick – get the tarpaulin up there,' hissed Jenny urgently.

Clumsily Andrew picked up the unwieldy tarpaulin, dropped it, picked it up again and somehow dragged it up to Jenny. But as he struggled Andrew was riveted by the expression he had seen in Brock's eyes. He had never witnessed such fear and despair in any human being. Brock had smelt of stale clothes and sweat and confinement and his hair and beard seemed even greyer than Andrew remembered them. And Brock was Jenny's father – it was unbelievable.

Somehow they managed to drape the tarpaulin over the cart before a furious Billy arrived back from The Packhorse.

'There's no bleedin' rope there!'

'Sorry,' said Jenny. 'I just remembered – I put it back in the shed in case Dad was angry.'

'You what?' Billy was really livid now. 'I've searched right through the kitchen and you've just remembered you put it back!'

'Too bad,' said Jenny ruthlessly and looked hard at Andrew. Suddenly he knew that they had to get rid of Billy at all costs.

'What?' asked Billy belligerently. 'What did you say?'

'Too bad. Andy, get the rope from the shed, will you?'

Billy turned on his heel. 'If you think I'm going to help you two idiots, you can think again.'

'Bye bye, Billy,' said Jenny calmly and infuriatingly. 'Go on, Andrew, hurry up.'

'Drop off!' replied Billy, turning back to the pub in a rage. 'I hope that nag bolts.'

'Then we'll get there quicker, won't we?' Andrew heard Jenny retort as he fumbled in the darkened shed for the rope. The small claustrophobic space smelt of Brock and his captivity.

After a frantic search he discovered the coil of rope on a hook and hurried out to Jenny. She was back on top of the cart, the sun catching her pale face in a golden glow. She looked like a triumphant goddess.

'Is that tight enough?'

'It'll have to do.'

Jenny took the reins and Andrew got up on the box beside her.

'Let's go.'

They clattered along the roadway, the contents of the shallow cart bouncing around inside. Andrew looked at his watch. It was 10.20 and already the road was full of traffic, which was being slowed down considerably by their stately progress.

'Good boy,' said Jenny to the horse. 'Gittup there, Brownie.' But the horse plodded on at a funereal pace and the fumes of the traffic around them became more and more intense.

'Blimey,' said Andrew. 'Are we allowed to hold the traffic up like this?'

'We're a vehicle, aren't we?' shouted Jenny above the thrumming of the engines. 'We've got a right to the public highway as well.' Andrew could see that there was no stopping her.

The horse and cart ambled slowly along in the choking heat until, thankfully, they came to a lay-by.

'Come on, Brownie.' With calm authority Jenny negotiated them into the litter-strewn space which ended in a clump of thick foliage. She reined in the horse, jumped off the box and ran to the rear of the cart. There she waited, watching the traffic carefully until there was a break in its ever-flowing stream. Then she ripped at one of the loosely tied ropes and an area of tarpaulin hung away.

'Now,' she hissed.

Brock leapt from the cart, like a terrified animal who could turn and then – Andrew did not like to think what Brock would do at bay. He knew instinctively that it would be something dreadful. Yet his helplessness was so awful that Andrew wanted to reach out and touch him.

Brock paused on the broken concrete of the lay-by, looked at Jenny for a moment, kissed her, ran his hand through Andrew's hair and dashed off into the foliage.

'The rope,' said Jenny. 'Quick.'

Andrew did up the trailing rope and they both jumped back on to the box.

'Come on, Brownie,' whispered Jenny, pulling at the reins. 'Let's go.'

The old horse trotted along the lay-by, waited some time for a gap in the traffic and then ambled out into the road. Glumly the traffic began to pile up behind them again, but Andrew felt such a glorious sense of relief that he could have burst into song. When he glanced across at Jenny, however, he could see that there were angry tears glistening in her eyes.

Andrew squeezed her arm. 'He's got a good chance,' he said.

'He's got the chance of a hunted animal,' she replied fiercely, her voice tight clenched.

'Yes,' said Andrew. 'But they get away, don't they? Sometimes.'

A few minutes later they heard the sound of a police siren and the traffic began to pull over to the side of the road. At once, Andrew felt deeply afraid. Why had he allowed Jenny to dominate him like this? Why did he need to prove himself to her?

'Don't be afraid,' said Jenny, pressing his hand.

'I'm not,' said Andrew woodenly.

'After all – we've got nothing to hide now.'

The police came slowly up in the outside lane, saw them and a white glove motioned them into the side. Then the car pulled up in front of them, its lights flashing. Two policemen leapt out and one instantly went to the back of the cart and began to undo the rope around the tarpaulin.

'What's the matter?' asked Jenny.

'Routine check, miss.'

'What are you looking for?'

'Oh – this, that and the other. Not a good idea to take a cart on a busy road, is it, miss?'

· 'We're delivering jumble.'

'Couldn't you have used another kind of vehicle?'

'I like driving a horse and cart.'

'Well, I don't s'pose everyone likes queuing behind you. Ever thought of that?'

'We're not going far, just to Platts Cross.'

'That's another half mile.' He frowned. 'And then you're going to come back?'

'Well, yes.'

The policeman turned to his colleague, who had just joined him from the rear of the cart. He looked even younger, with skin like a baby's.

'O.K., Bob?'

'Yup.'

'Well on your way then. And don't make a habit of holding up the traffic.'

They got back into the big white police car and nosed into the traffic which waited respectfully for them. When they had gone, Jenny let out a big sigh of relief.

'They're gone,' she said. 'Those two obviously hadn't sussed out I was in the police station.'

'How did it all happen, Jenny?'

At first she looked as if she wasn't going to tell him.

'How did you know Brock was your father?' he persisted.

Then she gave in.

'I didn't know until he came.'

'What – to the copse?'

'He came looking for me.'

'But what about Uncle George?'

'It broke him up. He'd always known I wasn't his, but no one told me. Apparently he and Mum didn't have much of a marriage even then. But she hadn't started drinking and she met this bloke – Brock – my dad.'

'What was he doing?'

'He was a naturalist – I don't know how he earned his living. By teaching, I think. I can see why she loved him – it's the same way I love him. He's so full of the land and its creatures. It's as if he's – ' she hesitated – 'as if he's the loving earth.'

'Then – '

'He and Mum – they – they got together. But then Dad found out. He's very jealous. He threatened them and Mum – I think she was too scared to leave him. Brock went away while she was still carrying me.'

'But Billy – '

'He's Dad's boy. Can't you see?' She laughed, but without humour.

'Why did Brock come back?'

'He'd done something – stolen some money from where he was working. He got found out and ran back here.'

'That was daft, wasn't it?'

'I suppose so. I think he wanted to see what I

was like before he got caught. He didn't have anybody else. He'd never married or anything.'

'How did you meet him?'

'I wasn't getting on with Dad and I was terribly worried about Mum. She'd been drinking for a long time. I used to go for walks and I met him up by the copse. He talked about badgers.'

'Didn't you think – '

'He was a dirty old man?' She laughed. 'No. It was just like having a friend. Then he told me. I didn't believe him at first.'

'How did you prove it?'

'He wrote a note to Mum and I took it to her. She was terrified that Dad would find out.'

'But she told you.'

'Yes, she told me.'

'How did you feel?'

'Just curious at first. I'd always got on well with Dad. I mean, I love him. I still do.'

'But *he* knows about Brock, doesn't he?'

'Oh yes. Mum can't keep a secret, not in her state.'

'What did he say?'

'He blustered – forbade me to see him. But I think he was frightened.'

'But why didn't your dad shop him? He could have got rid of him that way.'

'Because I pleaded with him, and because he loves me. He wanted me to get tired of him, I think. That's the hardest thing about Dad. He loves me so. He'd do anything to make me happy.'

'And now?'

'Time's up, he reckons. But he'll leave it to the police now.'

'How weird that he didn't shop him in spite of everything.'

'I threatened to leave home.'

'But where would you go?'

'I don't know but he took it seriously. He had to get back at us. Somehow.'

'The badger digging?'

'I couldn't stop him doing that. He knew we loved them. And Dad was determined that if he couldn't destroy us, he'd destroy them. Now it's an obsession, I think. Mark you, he's been after badgers for years – it was a sport. Now it's revenge.'

2 'Can't I come?'

'No.'

'Why not?'

'I'm sorry, Andy.'

They were passing The Packhorse with the empty cart on their way to return it to the farm. It was almost lunch-time and Jenny was trying to make Brownie go as fast as possible, which was not very fast. Andrew, however, did not have his mind on lunch at all. He could only think of the morning's experiences and the extent to which Jenny had protected Brock.

'I think you should go back to your parents, Andrew. It's all out of control.'

'I don't want to.' Andrew only wanted to be with Jenny – wherever she went.

'You'll be in trouble with the police.'

'I don't care.'

'Your parents will.'

'I don't care about that either,' Andrew said firmly, trying to banish the picture of his parents' distress if he did get into trouble. 'You used me in the first place. I won't let you dump me,' he added.

Jenny frowned. 'You realise the danger.'

'Yes.'

'Andrew, I'm sorry.' Relief and pleasure surged through Andrew at her acquiescence.

'I can help you.' Andrew sounded desperate in his efforts to please her.

'How?'

'I don't know yet. But I will.'

'It's going to be unpleasant.'

'Never mind that. But you must tell me.'

'What? Tell you what?'

'Where he's gone.'

'To earth,' she replied. 'Like the badgers.'

Lunch was awful. Billy was sulky, and when no one bothered to try and coax him out of his mood he said aggressively to Andrew:

'I'm going out with my mates this afternoon. *You* can stay with her.' His tone was sneering but Andrew knew that Billy was feeling rejected and hurt. He felt sorry for him but there was nothing he could do.

'All right, I will.'

'And later on,' added Billy maliciously, 'we're going badger-digging, aren't we, Dad? Up at that copse.'

Uncle George had the newspaper propped up in

front of him as he had at breakfast. There was again no sign of Auntie Prim.

'They're still looking for that bloke.' He lowered the paper and stared at Jenny balefully. Andrew noticed that a definite change had come over Uncle George since the row last night. He had lost all his rough kindness and now seemed like a gigantic, brooding bear who could break out at any time.

'Aren't we, Dad?' persisted Billy. 'We're goin' diggin' later, aren't we?'

I don't suppose I'm being very grateful to him – not to someone who saved my life, thought Andrew. But there was nothing he could do. There was no part for Billy.

'Yes,' said Uncle George softly, looking again at Jenny, 'we're going digging later, son.' He seemed almost to have forgotten Andrew's existence. 'And if we capture old Brock – ' Andrew saw Jenny start – 'I'm going to put him up against the dogs.'

'No!' Jenny screamed.

'Oh yes. And we're gonna take a few little bets in the yard tonight.'

Jenny's face slowly flushed and Billy seized his opportunity.

'Look at that – she's blushing.'

'Shut up!' said Andrew.

'All right, Andy. Don't get mixed up in family rows if you know what's good for you.'

'Sorry, Uncle George.' Andrew tried to sound contrite.

'Dad – you wouldn't.'

'It's time we flushed out a badger,' he replied stonily. 'Look what that big brute did to Trouncer.'

'That was in self-defence.'

'They don't always do things in self-defence,' said Uncle George. 'Sometimes they attack.'

'Only the odd baby rabbit.'

'Yes,' said Uncle George, 'that's it. And who's to protect the baby rabbits?'

'Don't be idiotic, Dad. You can't interfere with the laws of nature. What do they say – red in tooth and claw?'

But Andrew knew that Uncle George wasn't thinking about the laws of nature.

The argument continued throughout lunch with Billy alternately sulking and taunting while Jenny and Uncle George gave no ground to each other at all.

'Well, what *will* you do this afternoon, Andy?'

'He can't come with me,' said Billy abruptly.

'That's not a good way to treat our guest.' Uncle George tried to sound admonishing but failed. He now seemed to be totally obsessed with his hatred for the badgers.

'I'll take him,' said Jenny. 'We'll go for a walk.'

Billy whistled. 'Fancy him, do you?'

At last this was too much for Uncle George. 'Mind your lip, boy, or I'll give you a bang you'll never forget.'

'Sorry, Dad,' said Billy quickly, but Andrew knew that he did not mean it.

'And don't you go looking for the Gypo,' said Uncle George, 'or you'll be arrested.'

Jenny sighed. 'I'm sure there are enough people looking for him already.'

'Haven't you forgotten something?' asked Uncle George in a menacing voice.

'Forgotten what?' She had half risen from the table.

'My name.'

'Your name?'

'Yes.'

'Your name is Lammas. George Lammas.' Her voice was like ice.

'I'm your dad.'

Andrew saw that Billy was gazing curiously at both of them and Jenny caught Andrew's eye. Slowly she said:

'Sorry.'

The afternoon sky was overcast and the heat was sultry, thundery. Both Jenny and Andrew felt exhausted as they walked up the narrow road with its high banks and sweet-smelling wild flowers. Andrew could see that Jenny was deeply unhappy and he longed to say or do something that would cheer her up. But there was nothing that he could think of and he could have kicked himself in anger and frustration. All he could actually ask her was:

'Where is he?'

'In the copse.'

'That's mad.'

'Is it?'

'They'll come back to look.'

'And they won't find him.'

'Why?'

'Because he's well hidden – too bloody well hidden.'

'What about food?'

'That's the problem. He's good at foraging though.'

'He'll have to be. Shouldn't we have smuggled some food in from The Packhorse?'

'Just what *he*'ll be looking for.'

'Aren't you going to call Uncle George Dad any longer?'

'I shall try not to.' Her voice shook.

'Won't that be strange, after all this time?'

'I want to get used to it,' Jenny spoke so softly that Andrew could hardly hear her.

'I still think it's crazy that he's up in the copse. Or are you still choosing obvious places on purpose?'

Jenny kept glancing behind them as they walked. 'You wait till you see the hide.'

'No one's following us.'

'Not that we can see.'

'Who are you thinking of? The police? Uncle George?'

'I'm thinking of Billy.'

'He guesses?'

'Some of it – he's not an idiot.' She paused and glared angrily at Andrew. 'I'm not enjoying this, you know.'

'I didn't say you were.' Andrew was immediately defensive.

'I love Billy and Mum and even *him*. But I won't let them take my dad away.'

Andrew suddenly said: 'Supposing they did.'

'What do you mean?' she asked suspiciously.

'Well, supposing they caught him. He'd do his time and come out. Still your dad. After all, if he's done wrong – '

'I've thought about that,' said Jenny. 'But I don't think he'd be able to live in captivity.'

'What do you mean?'

'He's been in the wild too long.'

'On the run?'

'Yes, and before that. He's always been close to freedom. Animal freedom. I think he'd die.'

Andrew said nothing; she had convinced him.

'He hurt a policeman,' he burst out suddenly.

'That makes it worse. They'll give him longer.'

'He can't live in the copse for ever.'

'No. He's going to try and get abroad.'

'But you won't see him then.'

'I'll go to him. He'll send for me.' Her voice was confident, and Andrew could detect no hint of doubt.

'How will he get abroad?'

'I don't know. Yet.'

'He'll need money.'

'I know.'

'Well?'

'I know where Brock can get money. At least enough to cross the channel.'

'Where?'

'*He's* got a lot in the safe. *He* doesn't go to the bank till Monday.'

'You can't take it,' said Andrew, horrified.

'I can – I will take it.'

'Do you love him *that* much?'

'Yes, I do. Whatever Brock's done. You don't know what it's been like at home. *He* beats Mum, you know. And she's drinking more than ever.'

'Let's go and talk to Brock.'

'I don't want you.'

'I'm in now, Jenny. You *can't* get rid of me.'

She stood in the roadway, staring at him angrily. 'If you let me down – '

'Come on,' said Andrew, 'let's go.' But he was afraid. It wasn't just that he was terrified of Jenny's plan. There was something else. Eventually he realised what it was. He was uneasy about Brock. Was he manipulating Jenny?

The sky was darker and more overcast when they arrived at the copse. Coming from the far side they had climbed a high ridge and ran down the hill. The air was heavy and they did not speak. The trees in the copse were swathed in shadows and the musty tang of the badgers seemed to extend to the entire copse, making the tiny woodland smell acrid.

Jenny put a finger to her lips and walked through the trees softly as Andrew cautiously followed. Then she paused by what looked like the remains of a fallen tree trunk. She leant over it, went down on her knees and tapped on the wood. Immediately a piece of ground nearby slid back and Andrew saw a pair of scuffed hands with filthy fingernails. Then Brock's matted hair appeared and a few seconds later his exhausted-looking eyes. It was a particularly clever hiding place, well away from the badger sett – a sort of burrow which was held together by planks of wood and had a sliding wooden hatch on the top. This was covered by earth and foliage. Once shut, all evidence of it was concealed.

Brock scrambled out, covered in bits of earth and leaves. He shook himself down like an old dog and stretched out his long, gawky frame. Leaning forward he kissed Jenny.

'Hallo, love.'

'Hallo, Dad.'

Andrew looked down into the hole that Brock had left. It was minute and would only accommodate him. Andrew thought it was horribly like a grave. Then Brock turned to him.

'Still with us, eh?' But his voice was welcoming.

'He's been a help,' said Jenny softly.

'You know what kind of risk you're running, son.'

'Yes.'

'O.K. then. I'm grateful.' He grinned. 'I'm not innocent, you know.'

'Did you hurt the copper?'

Brock replied a little uncertainly: 'I hope not. I bashed him – first time I've ever hit anyone. But I had to get out.'

'What will you do?'

'If I can get to France – I've got a chance. But it's a long way overland.'

'When will you go?'

'Tonight – if I can.'

'She's going to steal money for you.'

'I'm afraid so.' He sounded apologetic but he didn't look particularly sorry.

'You don't think it would be better – ' But even as he spoke he saw an angry glint in Brock's eyes and his sense of unease increased.

'I'd go down for a long time. Two offences – could be five years. I wouldn't last six months.' He looked around the copse and added, very quietly, very firmly: 'I can't be locked up, you see.'

'But Jenny – and the money – '

'We're going to make it look as if I took it.'

'How?' said Andrew baldly.

Brock took a small crucifix from round his neck and showed it to Andrew. 'She's going to leave this – and this.' He bent over the hide and took out an iron wrench. It was enclosed in a polythene bag. 'It's got my fingerprints on it.'

'Isn't it very risky?' asked Andrew.

'Yes,' said Brock. 'But I must be free. I'm sorry.'

'If you can bring it tonight,' he pleaded, 'say before nine. Then I can move across country at night. I'll lie up during the day and make my way to the coast as fast as I can. I'll get a shave, some new clothes – and chance my luck.'

He looked at Andrew hesitantly and Andrew realised that Brock, if not afraid of him, was cautious. He obviously thought he didn't have his total loyalty. 'I've still got an up-to-date passport and if they haven't alerted the ports I might just make it.'

'They're coming here later,' said Jenny suddenly.

'Who?' He was immediately tense.

'Uncle George, Billy – the rest of the gang.'

'Digging?'

'Yes, I don't think even the hide's safe.'

'No.' Brock thought for a few seconds, his hands running nervously through his unkempt beard. 'Damn – the police will be out looking. I'll have to risk it. I built it to be undetectable by anyone. After all, the police missed it.'

'You think it's worth the risk?' Jenny asked anxiously.

He shrugged. 'I've got nowhere else to go.' Then he added: 'What are they going to do? Have another go at digging one out?'

'More than that. He's threatening to make it fight the terriers in the back yard. He said he'd got friends coming – that they wanted to place bets.'

'The bastard!'

'It's to get back at us.'

'I know. But he enjoys it anyway.'

'What are you going to do about the badgers?' Andrew's voice was stern.

Jenny stared at him hopelessly. 'I'm going to fight for them.'

'You'll draw attention to Brock if you do.'

'How?'

'Well, the more of a scene you make in this glade, the more chance they have of finding him.'

'He's right,' said Brock slowly.

'Then – ' she paused. 'What am I to do?'

'You've got a choice,' said Andrew. 'You can either defend the badgers or Brock. You can't defend them both.' He turned to Brock, seeking his reaction. But there was none – only a dogged determination to lie low until he could escape.

'I'm safe in the hide, love,' said Brock. 'Just for a while. Until you come back with the money.'

'But the badgers – ' She sounded confused.

'It's them or me.' His voice trembled a little and Andrew felt confused. Why was Brock suddenly so intent on his own survival? Didn't he care for the badgers any longer? Or was he just cornered?

'But I don't see it,' said Jenny. 'Why can't I protect the badgers? You'll be safe in your hole.'

'The dogs will smell me out.'

'So I'm to let them dig – and do nothing – '

'They probably won't get them anyway. Think what happened to the terrier.

Jenny hesitated.

'What's the time?' asked Brock quickly.

'Four,' said Andrew.

'You'd better get going. If they see you here – '

'O.K.' Jenny sounded weary. 'You'll be all right, won't you?'

'I'll be fine. You'll be back with the money by nightfall, won't you?'

'Yes.'

'Take these.' He put the crucifix into the polythene bag with the wrench. 'Don't touch them – remember they're covered with my fingerprints.' He turned to Jenny again and kissed her. 'We can trust Andrew to keep mum, can't we?'

'Yes,' said Jenny. 'You can trust him.'

'Go now – quickly.'

As they began to retrace their steps, Jenny looked back, but of Brock there was no sign. He had gone to earth.

3 They could hear Auntie Prim moving about upstairs at The Packhorse but Uncle George and Billy were out.

'They've gone up to the copse,' said Jenny in a strained voice.

'He's well hidden,' replied Andrew.

'Who?' she asked wildly and he stared at her puzzled.

'Brock of course – who do you think I'm talking about?' He realised she had been thinking of the badgers.

Somehow the hours passed but Jenny and Andrew

could concentrate on nothing. They made tea, watched some television and talked sporadically. All the time Andrew's concern for Jenny grew as she became more and more pale and tense.

'Are you really going to take the money?' he asked quietly as he watched her hands plucking at the tablecloth, picking distractedly at the edges while she gazed sightlessly at the television.

'Of course.' Her voice was just a little uncertain and Andrew wondered if she was having any doubts about Brock. After all he was betraying the badgers to save his own skin. But when Andrew saw the expression on her face, he knew she was still determined to go ahead.

'How much is in there?'

'Couple of hundred.'

'How will you get into it?'

'We all know the combination – it's been the same for years.'

'But – '

'I've got to do it, Andrew.' Her voice was rigid and he was afraid to push her any further.

They continued to stare at the television, each listening to their own thoughts – Jenny with her obsessive determination and Andrew with his fears for her.

'When will he send for you?' said Andrew eventually, desperate to break the silence that had become a wall between them.

'When he's ready.'

There was a long pause and then Jenny suddenly stood up.

'It's pointless waiting any longer. I'm going to take the money now.'

'What if Uncle George comes back and checks?'
'We'll just have to hope he doesn't.'
'What's the time?'
'Six. There was no point in waiting in the first place. It'll only be more difficult when *he's* here. I can give Dad the money earlier.'
'You watch you don't run into Uncle George and Billy on their way back.'
She paused. 'Andy – '
'Yes?'
'Help me – I'm scared.'
Proudly Andrew followed her.

The safe was on the top floor of The Packhorse, standing on a chest of drawers near what must have originally been a maid's room.
'Where's your mum?' hissed Andrew nervously.
'Where else? In her room – laid out.'
Jenny approached the safe confidently, drew on a pair of gloves and began to fiddle with the combination. After dialling various digits, the door creaked open to reveal bunches of notes held together by elastic bands. There was a leather purse inside the safe and Jenny pulled it out, stuffing the notes inside.
The theft was over in a couple of minutes and as Jenny noiselessly closed the door, Andrew felt a burning sense of relief. Somewhere, at a great distance, a voice kept drumming away in his head, talking about stealing and the police and what his parents would think, but it was as if it were wrapped in cotton wool, for it had only a muffled impact on him.
Jenny stood hesitantly in front of the closed safe,

holding the bag, and Andrew wondered if she was hearing the same kind of voice. Then she turned abruptly away, slipping the purse into an old carrier-bag that was lying on the landing amongst some newspapers.

But as they hurried downstairs a door opened and Auntie Prim stood on the threshold. She looked haggard in the fading light of the summer's evening, but she certainly did not look drunk.

'Where are you going?' she asked.

Trapped, Jenny stopped beside her mother, giving her a peck of a kiss on her dry cheek. 'We thought we heard mice.'

'Mice! There's been mice up there for years. What are you up to?'

'Honest, Mum – nothing.'

'What's in that bag?'

'Some books I rescued from the jumble.'

'We don't want more rubbish in this house.'

Jenny made as if to hurry on, but Auntie Prim stood in the way. She looked at Andrew.

'Are you having a nice time?'

'Yes, thank you,' he replied politely.

'Where are you going?'

He gaped at her for a moment, unable to think of anything. Then he stuttered: 'We're going to watch TV.'

'A nice cosy evening,' Auntie Prim agreed.

'We're tired,' said Jenny.

Auntie Prim made a sudden decision. 'I'll join you,' she said enthusiastically. 'I haven't watched TV in months. What's on?' They were both stumped for a reply but Auntie Prim did not seem to need an answer. 'I expect there's something good on a Sunday.' She began to walk down the stairs and they meekly followed her.

'What are we going to do?' hissed Andrew.

'What's that?' asked Auntie Prim.

Jenny winked desperately at Andrew and he knew that her mind was racing, trying to think of a way out.

Gradually Andrew began to wonder about Auntie Prim's sudden interest in television. Could she be trying to keep them by her? Did she guess what they had done or did she actually know? Either way she sat very close to them whilst they watched a Western, and every time either of them moved she turned and smiled.

Eventually Jenny said: 'I'm just going to the loo, Mum.'

'Don't be long, dear. This *is* exciting, isn't it?'

'Yes,' said Andrew, feeling a reply was expected. He knew that Jenny was going back upstairs to plant the wrench by a window and the crucifix in some other incriminating position. Then the job would be complete – and they should be free to go. But the carrier-bag full of money lay under Jenny's chair and Auntie Prim was clearly determined that they should sit with her.

'She's a long time,' began Auntie Prim, but luckily Jenny came in almost immediately and, slightly breathless, slumped in front of the TV. Was she thinking the same thing that Uncle George would be back soon and might wonder what was in that bag.

Meanwhile the bar had opened, and one of Uncle George's stand-ins was playing mine host to the usual desultory Sunday evening crowd. The situation seemed to have reached deadlock until to Andrew's relief he saw his aunt close her eyes, yawn and then close her eyes again.

For a few minutes they sat, transfixed, staring at Auntie Prim as she slept while the TV rustlers shot the TV sheriff. Andrew could no longer see the pictures on the screen. All he could see was an image of Jenny standing with her father in the copse and the badgers snuffling round their feet. Then he saw a line of policemen advancing on them in the dark – a line that was headed by Uncle George, a lantern in one hand and a pair of badger tongs in the other.

Taking another look at his aunt now gently snoring, Andrew hissed at Jenny: 'Get going!'

Towards the end of the film Uncle George and Billy came home. Uncle George went straight into the bar and Billy joined them round the screen. He was in a very good mood and all his old sulkiness and jealousy seemed to have disappeared. Andrew longed to ask him how he had got on, but they watched the television screen in silence until the film ended. Auntie Prim was still asleep as Andrew turned to Billy and asked impatiently:

'Well?'

'What?' Billy grinned at him as he had done on their first meeting at the railway station – with a challenge.

'How did you get on?'

'No go.'

'You didn't get one.'

'No.' He sighed and grinned again. 'Gave us the slip.'

'Dogs all right?'

'Yeah – they're fine. No more blood.' He yawned. 'I'm knackered. Where's Jenny?'

'She went to see some friends,' he said without a pause.

'Who?'

'I don't know.'

'Isn't that great – leaving you on your own.'

'I don't mind. I've been watching TV with your mum.'

'I bet she's gone to that stuck-up Susan – just down the road.'

'Maybe.'

'Do you want some coke – there's some in the fridge?'

'O.K.'

'I'll get it then I'm going to bed. I feel done in.'

'Me too.'

Billy left the room and Andrew let out a sigh of relief. Maybe Jenny would get away with it after all. He wondered, however, how quickly Uncle George would discover the money was missing.

Andrew was awakened by the strangest noise he had ever heard. It was a kind of weird howling that made him sit bolt upright. It was repeated again – and again – and again. Then there was silence.

After a while the terriers began to bark, as if they had not dared to make a sound during the howling. But even their barking had a fearful note, as if they sensed something alien in their surroundings.

For a while Andrew could not work out if he had

been dreaming or not and as the howl was not repeated, he assumed he must have been. Gradually the barking died away and he drifted off to sleep again.

The next morning all hell broke loose when Uncle George took the night's takings to the safe. Andrew was woken by his angry shouts and as he was getting out of bed Billy rushed into his room.

'Guess what?'

'What?'

'The old Gypo's burgled the house.'

'Who?'

'You know – the old Gypo who used to fancy Jenny.'

'Him!'

'He got in during the night. He could have killed us as we slept.' Billy fully appreciated the melo-dramatic situation.

'What's he done?' yawned Andrew, looking at his watch. It was 8 a.m. and he saw that Billy was dressed in his school clothes.

'He's nicked the weekend's take. Dad's going mad.'

'Blimey.'

'But he's left some stuff behind – they'll have his fingerprints unless he's been smart.'

Billy's excitement knew no bounds and Andrew tried to sound interested.

'What a nerve coming here,' said Billy.

'Are you sure it was him?'

'Who else would want money fast? Dad's called the coppers. They'll be here in a sec. We're not to touch nothing.'

Andrew said: 'I'd best get some clothes on.'

'Yeah, Jenny's getting breakfast.'

So she was all right. Andrew almost breathed an audible sigh of relief but stopped himself just in time.

'I'll be down,' he said.

'You encouraged that bastard!'

'Oh shut up.' Jenny sounded exhausted as she battled with an enormous frying pan.

'Now he's nicked the take.' Uncle George sounded more hurt than angry, as if the invasion of his property had left some kind of taint. Suddenly Andrew no longer felt afraid of his uncle, for despite his massive size and obvious strength he seemed a pathetic figure today.

'How much did he take, Dad?'

''Bout three hundred.'

'And he got in by the landing window?'

'Shinned up the bathroom roof and up to the window.'

'I heard the dogs barking,' said Billy. 'But I thought it was the – ' He stopped and looked at Andrew and his father quickly interrupted, one eye on his daughter.

'They're always barking, that lot. Bloody hopeless guard dogs.'

There was a ring at the side-door bell.

'That'll be the police,' said Uncle George, levering himself to his feet. 'Now you get off to school, Billy boy, and you, Jen.'

As Billy went to get his bag Andrew had the opportunity to ask Jenny quickly:

'How did it go? Did you give it to him?'

'Yes.' She sounded almost relaxed.

'And he got away?'

'I saw him go over the hillside. I waited until he was out of sight.'

'Did he say anything?'

'Oh yes.' Her radiance increased.

'What did he say?'

'He kept saying it.' She seemed almost bemused with happiness, staring into the distance as she spoke.

'*What* did he say?' persisted Andrew impatiently.

'He said he'd send for me. Oh Andrew – ' She lightly kissed Andrew on the forehead and slipped out of the room.

When the policeman came into the kitchen, both Billy and Jenny had gone to school. Uncle George followed him in, looking tired.

'Your wife wouldn't have heard anything?'

'She sleeps like a log, but you're welcome to talk to her. I'll get her up.'

'No, let her sleep on.'

'I told you she was a bit of an invalid.'

'Yes, sir. I'll see her presently. And who is this young man?'

'This is Andrew, my sister-in-law's boy.'

'You hear anything, Andrew?'

'Just some barks.'

'Anything else?'

He thought of the howl but said nothing. 'No.'

'No scrabbling about?'

'No, nothing at all.'

'O.K., son.' The policeman looked about him as if to ensure all was well – at least in the room.

Uncle George said: 'You've had plenty of men out looking for him, haven't you?'

'All night,' said the policeman. He was middle-aged and respectful yet Andrew noticed there was a lassitude about him, as if he was not really interested in his job – let alone having the 'Gypo' caught. 'And no sign yet. He's gone to earth somewhere, but he must have been desperate, sneaking in like this.' The policeman cleared his throat, as if making conversation. 'The C.I.D. will be here shortly.'

But this was not good enough for Uncle George. 'You've got men out this morning, haven't you? I mean – he's got my money.'

'We've got an all-car alert, sir, and they're combing the hills again.'

Uncle George grunted and Andrew felt a rush of sympathy for him. There had not been any evidence of police activity when he and Jenny had gone to Brock's hiding place yesterday afternoon.

Uncle George turned to Andrew. 'And what have you got planned for today, Andy?'

'I thought of exploring – ' His voice tailed off.

'I wouldn't advise that,' said the policeman. 'You don't want to go wandering about the countryside, Andrew. This man's dangerous. He already knows your cousin – and that's why he came here.'

Uncle George shot the policeman a glance of barely concealed contempt at this brilliant deduction.

'Tell you what, you hang around until the C.I.D.'s been and then you can come into Taunton with me. I've got some supplies to pick up. O.K.?'

'O.K., Uncle George.' Andrew heard the dogs

barking again and was reminded of the howls he had heard last night.

'Those dogs kick up a racket,' said the policeman
'They're hungry,' said Uncle George. 'I'd better go and feed them.'

'Well, lad? It's been quite hectic, hasn't it?'

Andrew nodded as Uncle George drove his old pick-up truck rattling down the road to Taunton.

'I don't s'pose you expected your visit to be as – as exciting as this, did you?'

'No, Uncle George.'

'You know – ' the empty pipe waggled in his mouth furiously as he changed gear – 'we may have a lot of arguments, us Lammases, a lot of aggro as young Billy would say, but we're all together. Course my wife's a bit of an invalid. And Jenny, well Jenny's headstrong. But Billy, he's the sanest of us all. I hope you're enjoying yourself.' His voice was suddenly almost wistful, with a strange yearning in it that Andrew found moving. 'You're Billy's mate, I know. A few scraps, of course, but he's a good boy is Billy. You like my Billy, don't you Andy?'

'Yes, he's great.'

'Now Jenny, she's a real little madam. As you can see, we're not always eye to eye. But she's my girl, you know. She's my girl.'

Andrew didn't know what to make of this comment so he kept quiet.

'She's a lovely girl is Jenny.' Uncle George sounded as if he was thinking aloud. 'She don't agree with my badger hunting though.'

'Why *do* you do it, Uncle George?' asked Andrew.

'You don't like it either. I know that, Andy.'

'But why – why do you do it?' Andrew insisted.

Uncle George drew at his empty pipe and once again Andrew had the impression that he was thinking aloud. 'Why? Damned if I know. Always done it.'

'Jenny – she hates it.'

'I don't like being told what to do – and what not to do. See.'

'You mean you do it because she tells you not to.'

'Now, Andy, don't start getting deep. I can't take it. Badger digging's part of the old ways, and they're my ways. I won't be told to alter them – whatever she says.' His voice was fierce but then he added more gently, 'She's my girl, though.' His knuckles whitened as he gripped the steering wheel, and for the first time Andrew realised how strongly, how passionately Uncle George felt about his family, about Jenny. Without thinking Andrew put his hand on his uncle's arm and rested it there for a second before he withdrew it.

'You're a good boy, Andy,' said Uncle George. But he did not relax.

Uncle George bought Andy lunch in Taunton after they had loaded numerous boxes of crisps and nuts from the Cash and Carry. They had a look round the town and Andrew sent a postcard to his parents which read: HAVING A SMASHING TIME – SEE YOU SOON.

Just before four they drove slowly home. It had been raining gently on and off and there was a fine spray on the road that kept misting the windscreen.

Then Andrew noticed a rainbow shimmering amongst the rain clouds.

'There's a crock of gold at the bottom of that lot,' said Uncle George so quietly that Andrew could only just make out the words.

'Shall we find it?' asked Andrew, not really knowing what else to say.

'Not if I'm with you, lad,' he whispered back. 'My luck's out.'

4 The men began arriving at six and soon the car park of The Packhorse was full. Bewildered, Andrew asked Billy what they had come for and received a casual, yet somehow uneasy reply.

'There's gonna be one of Dad's auctions.'

'Auctions?'

'Bits of farming equipment. Motors. That kind of thing.'

'I don't see any equipment.'

'It's all in the cars and vans. Small stuff, mark you.'

'Are you going to it?'

'Might as well. But you won't like it.'

'Why not?'

'It's boring. Dad said you might like to catch the bus into Taunton tonight and see a film with Jenny. *E.T.*'s on.'

'But I've been in Taunton all day with Uncle George. He didn't say anything about the film.'

'Kept it as a surprise. He'll give you some money.'

'Does Jenny know?'

'She's not home yet.'

When Jenny arrived home, she was far from keen and she turned on Billy irritably.

'I'm knackered. Doesn't he know I've had a hard day at school – *and* I had to stay behind for athletics.'

'He thought it would be a treat.'

Then Uncle George came in from the bar.

'Jenny – I'm going to give you ten quid. Take Andrew into Taunton to see *E.T.* and have a snack afterwards. Then you can just catch the last bus.'

'I'm tired.'

'It doesn't matter, Uncle George,' said Andrew hastily. 'I'd just as soon stay at home and watch your auction.'

Jenny shrugged. 'There you are.'

'We have a guest, Jenny. We should entertain him.'

'I've never known you to have an auction on a Monday. You never mentioned it before.'

'I forgot – and I don't want Andy bored.'

'I won't be bored, Uncle.'

'And I say you will.' He sounded quite angry now and was glaring at Jenny. 'Haven't you brought me enough trouble, girl, without causing any more?'

'I'm not causing any – '

'You'll entertain our guest.' The statement was final and Jenny reluctantly gave in.

'All right,' she said. 'We'll go to Taunton.'

★

As they stood at the bus stop in the dank coolness of the rainwashed evening, Jenny suddenly said:

'Oh, no!'

'What's the matter?'

She stood there as if transfixed by a thought that deeply grieved her and there was a dead look in her eyes.

'We've been conned.'

'What are you on about?'

She rounded on him, her eyes blazing into a furious anger.

'I'm on about what they're up to, the bloody liars!'

Andrew continued to gaze blankly at Jenny and she gave him an impatient, almost hostile look.

'Don't you understand?'

'No.'

'They got a badger last night – they got one.'

'But they said – '

'To hell with what they said!'

Andrew remembered the terrible howling he had heard in the night. His mind refused to accept that it had been a badger yet he could see in Jenny's eyes that it must be true.

'How could they do it?'

'They've done it.'

'I must have heard it crying out last night. Poor thing. But what for?'

'You idiot,' she stormed. 'Don't you know why all those men have come? They've brought it back from the copse – to fight the terriers.'

'No – '

'*Yes*, Andrew,' she said bitterly. 'Those men have come to watch the fight. To watch and to place bets.

And *he's* sent us to the cinema so that we won't know. It's his final revenge against my father.'

'He loves you, Jenny.' The words seemed forced out of him.

'Don't say any more.' She began to stride away.

'Where are you going?'

'There's a telephone box up the road. I'm going to use it.'

'Who are you going to phone?'

'The police, of course.'

'Shall I come with you?'

'No.' She paused to think. 'Try and sneak back into the pub and go up to my room. Make sure you're not seen.'

'Then what do I do?'

'On my dressing-table there's a camera. It's loaded with film. Do you know how to use it?'

'You bet.'

'Go round the back by the shed where Brock hid and walk across the allotment. There's a wall between the allotment and the yard and another old shed. Hide behind it. They'll all be in the yard. Try and get some photos of what they're doing – just in case no one believes me.'

'I'll get as many as I can,' he said, but Jenny didn't seem to hear him.

'Andrew – this is cruel. Do you understand? It's filthy cruelty.' She was beginning to gabble and there was a rising note of hysteria in her voice as if she was losing control of herself. 'That bastard – he's doing it for Brock. Don't you see – to him that badger's Brock.' She began to laugh and the loud, raucous sound quickly dissolved into tears of rage and sorrow. Andrew walked towards Jenny in an attempt to comfort her, but she backed away, raising her arms as if he was going to attack her.

'Don't touch me.'

'Jenny – '

'Just do what I say.'

'I want to do it anyway,' said Andrew. 'You don't have to tell me to do it.'

'Then get on with it.' She turned on her heel and began to run off down the road. As Andrew cautiously started to walk back to The Packhorse he could hear Jenny sobbing.

The pub was deserted as Andrew tiptoed inside, but he could hear a great deal of noise coming from the yard. The cheering and booing rose in waves of harsh sound and he could not bear to think what was happening out there. Hurriedly he ran upstairs to Jenny's room and opened the door. The camera was lying on her dressing-table and he snatched it up, his hand trembling. It looked fairly similar to his father's and he knew how to work that all right, but how was he going to get near enough to get the photos? Would they see him? These and dozens of other questions raced across his mind as he closed the door of Jenny's room and began to tiptoe down the stairs again. When he was just half-way down he heard a rustling on the landing. Andrew looked up and saw Auntie Prim standing there, watching him. He was so startled that he almost dropped the camera.

'Andrew?'

'Yes?' he whispered.

'Where are you going?' Her voice was shrill but she seemed to be quite sober.

'I – I – ' he stuttered.

'George said that you and Jenny were going to the pictures.'

'I know. We – we changed our minds.'

'Why?'

Andrew said nothing, his mouth opening and closing like a goldfish. Then they both heard a renewed burst of shouting and cheering from outside.

'That's why,' said Andrew.

She gazed at him, not understanding.

'The badger. They're making it fight one of the dogs.'

'I know,' she said flatly and Andrew stared up at her, surprised.

'Jenny – Jenny's phoning the police,' he blurted out.

'Well,' Auntie Prim sighed. 'Maybe she's right. But of course he's really laying him to rest.'

So his aunt had been aware of everything all the time.

'He's gone,' he said. 'At least – ' He broke off, not sure even now whether she was referring to Brock or to the captive badger. Then he realised that she was in fact talking about both.

'Yes.' Her voice was hard. 'I've no doubt he's gone. He got what he wanted.'

'But he's going to send for Jenny.'

'Him? He's off. He won't be back.'

'I know. He can't come back.' Andrew sounded desperate. 'But he's going to send for her.'

'Like he was going to send for me. But he never bloody did. Now George is laying him to rest.'

'But that's not Brock – it's a badger.'

'They're both the same to your Uncle George.'

'You're all rotten,' yelled Andrew in sudden fury.

'Yes,' she agreed, 'we're all rotten. Rotten to the core.'

'I'll fix him,' shouted Andrew. 'Why should an animal have to suffer because of you lot?'

'Go and do what you can,' said Auntie Prim. 'Go and get on with it.'

Andrew went round the back of the pub and across the allotment to the shed. Its bulk separated him from the yard. Furtively he struggled behind it, working his way along its side which was covered with dusty foliage and cobwebs. Eventually he stood panting between a brick wall and the mildewed wood. At last he could see what was going on and the sight chilled him to the marrow.

The men in the yard had formed a half circle. Some were crouching and others were standing. In front of them crouched a bloodied dog. A few paces away, the badger was still, waiting and dominant. A sudden guilty pleasure seized Andrew. The badger was going to win. He did not know which of the terriers the injured dog was but when he glanced up he saw that Uncle George looked grey and strained, his eyes as full of pain as the terrier's. Then the dog drew back, eyeing the badger apprehensively as it poised to spring. After what seemed an interminable time the badger drove itself at the dog, biting upward as it lowered its head and charged. The terrier took the attack full in the face and seized the badger around the neck in its jaws. Andrew's heart pounded as the two animals were locked together still upright. Then, gradually, the terrier's grip weakened as the badger bit deep into his face. With a sobbing yowl it let go of the badger's neck, but the badger's jaws remained clamped around its nose.

Andrew felt the nausea rushing up from his stomach as the terrier slumped on to its back with the badger bearing down on top. Its yowls continued until they merged into one long-drawn-out shriek of pain. Andrew's eyes darted automatically to Uncle George's face, which was a replica of the agony. Then, with a gasping cry, Uncle George picked up a broken spar of wood and raised it high above his head. As he did so, Andrew could see the deadly spike of a nail sticking out from underneath the wood.

As if by instinct, Andrew picked up the camera and focused it on Uncle George. For a few seconds he held up the spar and Andrew watched the despair in his uncle's eyes. Then Uncle George brought the spike hard down on to the badger. At the last moment the striped body seemed to flinch sideways and the spar missed its head, driving deep into the body. At once, above the terrier's screaming, came a shriek of agony.

Andrew lowered the camera, conscious that he had pressed the shutter, but not knowing when he had done so. Numbly he saw Uncle George raise the spar again and watched tensely as the nail came out of the badger's fur. For a moment Andrew thought Uncle George was going to drive it in again for the badger's jaws were still firmly clamped around the terrier's nose, but suddenly it released its grip and rolled over. The two animals lay side by side, their bodies heaving, emitting two very different but equally unbearable cries.

Uncle George threw away his spar and knelt down by the terrier, not daring to touch its wounds but stroking its head lovingly, hopelessly. One of the men nearest him went over to comfort him. The badger lay on its side, its paws threshing the air, gradually quietening until it gave a squeaking noise.

At this pathetic, tremulous sound Andrew's shoulders heaved and he was sick. When he had finished, he felt very weak and leant back against the shed for support. When he managed to find strength to look again the scene had changed. The terrier was still crying but the badger was quiet now, its limbs twitching feebly. Uncle George was still kneeling by his dog but he was now looking up at a policeman, who was talking to him quietly. Jenny was standing by them and there was a man in a tweed suit, who was walking towards the badger, carrying a small bag.

Andrew caught sight of Billy for the first time, crouched at the back of the crowd, which moved forward towards Uncle George. He sat on the ground, not attempting to go near the animals, a small, miserable heap who stared ahead as if, like Andrew, he could no longer take in the situation.

Then Jenny yelled: 'Andrew!' At first he did not move but then she called again: 'Andrew.' Her voice was cold and commanding. Obediently, Andrew emerged from his hiding place, holding the camera. At first no one noticed him and it was not until he was standing by Uncle George and the bleeding terrier that Jenny said: 'Have you got it?'

Miserably he nodded and then another voice rapped out:

'Got what?' asked Billy who came up and when he saw the camera screamed at Andrew 'I'm gonna smash you,' he began, 'smash you so bloody hard –' But he made no move towards him.

'I took a photograph,' said Andrew woodenly.

'You'd better let me have the camera, son,' said the policeman. He had one hand on Uncle George's shoulder. 'You've made a mess of this, George,' he said quietly. 'A real mess.'

Billy asked: 'Why did you do it, Andy?'

'I had to,' Andrew replied and looked at Jenny. He noticed that she kept looking down at the badger but in a curious, dispassionate way as if she had already accepted the situation. The vet was bending over the still twitching body and he looked up at her.

'I can't do anything,' he said quietly. He got up and came over to the terrier. There were great gouges in its face and the blood was still welling up. He knelt down and after a few seconds said: 'He'll be O.K. – after I've patched him up.'

Jenny said: 'Will you do me a favour?'

The vet looked up. 'What's that, Jenny?'

'On the way back could you give me a lift?'

'Where to?'

'The layby on the Taunton Road.'

'Why do you want to go there?'

'It's not all that far from the sett.'

'But he's dying.'

'I know, but I want to take him back.' There was a new gentleness in her voice.

The vet hesitated. 'How are you going to – take him?'

'I'll carry him.'

'You'll never do it – he's too heavy.'

'I'll help,' said Billy. 'Will you let me help, Jen?'

She nodded and looked across at Andrew. 'Will you come too?'

'Yes.' He could not say any more for tears were streaming down his cheeks.

'I'll come with you, girl.' Andrew was startled to hear his uncle's voice.

'It's all right,' said Jenny softly, 'we can manage. You look after the dog.'

Uncle George nodded slowly and then Andrew saw another figure approaching. He could hardly recognise it at first. He saw a small woman in a red skirt and blouse. She looked homely, concerned and somehow deeply reassuring. It was Auntie Prim but for once Andrew could detect no smell of violets. She came briskly across and put her hands on Uncle George's shoulders, as he knelt by the softly whining terrier.

'You'd better come in,' she said. 'The vet will take him.' Auntie Prim looked up at the policeman. 'Do you need him any more?'

'There'll be more questions,' he began, and then added: 'but it'll do later.' He turned to the spectators: 'And you lot, get going, or you'll be nicked.' The crowd moved quickly away without looking back.

'Well – ' The vet paused. 'I'll back my van up. We can take them both together.

The vet's van drove slowly into the layby.

'Are you sure you can manage?'

'Yes,' said Jenny.

'I've got an old blanket, you can wrap him up in that.'

'Thanks.'

'And Jenny – '

'Yes?'

'Try not to take this too hard. I reckon your father's learnt his lesson.'

But she merely nodded impatiently and said to Billy and Andrew, who were sitting in the back of the van with the two animals: 'Come on, you boys. We've got work to do.'

5 It was almost half-past eight and dusk was still over an hour away. The badger was very heavy and they took turns to carry it, slowly plodding up the slope, their arms aching and their breath coming in short bursts. No one spoke as they staggered along in the still and humid air. Sweating profusely, Andrew wondered if the badger was already dead as it was so inert.

'Let's have a rest,' pleaded Billy.

'No,' said Jenny, taking over from him. 'Let me do the carrying.'

'But – '

'We've got to get him there before dusk. Before the others come.'

They walked on with Billy in the lead and

Andrew and Jenny supporting the badger. Andrew suddenly felt a small shudder of movement. 'He's still here.'

'I want him to know he's back in the copse,' said Jenny. There was no tremor in her voice. 'I want him to know he's home.'

The shadows lengthened as they travelled on until, gasping for air, they reached the top of the hill and the edge of the copse.

'Don't speak,' said Jenny. 'And tread quietly.'

'Where are we going to put him?' hissed Andrew.

'Just by the sett,' she replied. 'So they'll find him.'

Half an hour later, Jenny, Billy and Andrew stood behind the barbed wire, watching dusk slowly creep over the copse. The air was cooler now and Andrew felt a pervading sense of peace. The badger lay a few yards away, near one of the entrances to the sett. It was still alive, sometimes giving a little tremble. Andrew did not know if it was in pain. Perhaps Jenny had been wrong to bring it back, perhaps somebody should have killed it in the yard. But the vet had let them bring it back. He had said nothing so maybe it was all right.

'This is something,' whispered Billy.

'Shh,' admonished Jenny, but she did not sound cross.

'No, but it is,' he hissed unrepentantly. 'I wish I'd gone watching before.'

'Well, you didn't.'

Even Billy was quiet as the landscape was shrouded in the glowing dark. A tiny wind began to rattle the copse and it grew until it was blowing quite strongly. Suddenly Jenny stiffened and nudged Andrew, who nudged Billy. A dark shape had emerged from one of the entrances to the sett and had its head up to the wind, smelling the evening perfumes, checking to see whether all was safe. It was the sow, preceding her cubs. The boar lay at another entrance and she did not seem to have detected his presence.

They all waited, the tension creeping over them. A minute later they saw the cubs emerge from the sett and begin to gambol behind the sow. Suddenly she seemed to discover the presence of the boar and she scurried over to him, followed by the cubs. For a while they kept their distance and then they began to edge nearer, nosing at the still shape.

Around them the darkness closed in until the dusk had merged into night. Looking up above the trees Andrew saw the moon riding high over the ragged, trailing clouds. The copse was now lit by a pale light which silhouetted the badgers.

Suddenly Jenny gripped Andrew's arm so hard that it hurt and he could feel Billy tense beside him. The boar had raised its head. Just a little and with considerable effort. There was a whickering sound from the sow and a softer one, which Andrew thought perhaps had come from the boar, but he wasn't sure. He saw the head of the boar stiffen and then flop down.

Andrew continued to watch the glade, fully relaxed and calm. He sensed that Jenny and Billy, wedged in beside him, were feeling the same. The moon had passed behind swirling clouds and the copse was now in darkness, but they could still hear the badgers as they whickered in the blackness of the glade. The wind was sweeping through the trees and he could smell the musk of the badgers blown erratically towards him in fits and starts. Suddenly the whickering stopped and there was a scampering sound. Then there was silence.

Billy began to shiver.

'What's the matter?' asked Andrew.

'Someone's coming.'

'No.'

'The badgers have gone to earth,' said Jenny.

The clouds parted to allow more wan moonlight to flood the copse. Only the dead boar lay in front of the sett entrance – the other badgers had disappeared.

'There *is* someone,' said Billy.

Now they could hear footsteps in the undergrowth, slow and cautious.

'It must be Brock,' exclaimed Andrew, forgetting to whisper. 'He's come back, Jenny.'

'No,' she said. 'It won't be Brock.'

But Andrew was not listening. 'He's come back for you, Jenny! He's come back.'

'It's Dad,' said Billy.

George Lammas stood in the centre of the moonlit glade. He was wearing a huge sweater and this made him look bigger than ever in the distorted light.

'Jenny,' he whispered gently. 'Jenny.'

'Coming, Dad,' she answered. Jenny scrambled through the wire, leaving Billy and Andrew to watch as she ran into his arms. 'Take me home,' she said. She looked down at the boar and then buried her face in her father's sweater.